EROTICA

Here is a thoughtfully arranged and beautifully presented collection of sexual art and literature – the first of its kind in one volume. The range covers 2,000 years, from Classical Rome to the novels of D. H. Lawrence and Henry Miller.

The field of erotica is vast and varied, and the selections here are chosen not only to inform and entertain but also to excite. Care has been taken, however, to exclude pernicious, degrading or violent material. The emphasis is on the life-enhancing qualities of good erotica, and the result is a collection that will appeal as much to women as it does to men.

Sexually inspired images are among the earliest evidence of human culture – the 'Venus of Willendorf', a stone amulet from Austria, dates from 30,000 BC, and since then artists and authors from every culture and quarter of the globe have expressed their sexuality in a multitude of forms. The artist Eduard Fuchs said, 'Art has treated erotic themes at almost all periods, because eroticism lies at the root of all human life.'

Similarly, erotic literature speaks to the heart of human experience. Throughout history countless writers have disclosed their innermost thoughts and experiences, in fiction, poetry, drama, songs, letters and journals – whether intended to be freely circulated or produced for a select circle, depending on the climate of the times.

This anthology presents a stimulating range of the very best examples of erotic art and literature, with contributions from familiar names – Frank Harris, John Cleland, Anaïs Nin, Boccaccio, Casanova – as well as some surprises. Sometimes suppressed or frowned upon in their time, these works are presented here in celebration of the universal attraction of the erotic experience.

EROTICA

An Illustrated Anthology of
Sexual Art and Literature

Charlotte Hill
and
William Wallace

Carroll & Graf Publishers, Inc.
New York

First published in the United States in 1992 by
Carroll & Graf Publishers, Inc.

Carroll & Graf Publishers, Inc.
260 Fifth Avenue
New York, NY 10001

Library of Congress Cataloging-in-Publication-Data is available on request
from Carroll & Graf

ISBN 0–88184–874–3

AN EDDISON · SADD EDITION
Edited, designed and produced by
Eddison Sadd Editions Limited
St Chad's Court, 146B King's Cross Road
London WC1X 9DH

Phototypeset in Caslon ITC No 224 Book by
Dorchester Typesetting, Dorset, England
Origination, printing and binding by
Toppan Printing Company, Hong Kong

———— ◊ ————

FRONTISPIECE
Venus, the Love Goddess, who
epitomizes feminine beauty and
the erotic sentiment. Oil painting
on canvas by an unknown artist,
Netherlands, seventeenth century.

———— ◊ ————

Contents

INTRODUCTION

The maze

RIGHT Zeus, the male principle and Father of the Gods, on one of his frequent missions to that end. School of David, France, eighteenth century.

So far as we know, this is the first book of its kind: an illustrated anthology of erotica, taking as its source material the sexual art and literature of both East and West. We believe it is the first of its kind, but we are mindful of Marie Antoinette's milliner, who was moved to point out to her demanding client one day: 'Nothing is new, ma'am, only what has been forgotten.'

Human sexuality is a vast subject. Although it is only comparatively recently that our culture has come of age and decided that erotic literature can be made available to the general public, it has always been written, and the great libraries of the world have whole sections devoted to it. Erotic art, too, has always been produced – either for wealthy patrons or for the amusement of the artists themselves or their close circle – but has seldom seen the light of day. Even great art, even the religious icons of other cultures, will often languish unseen in the vaults of museums if it is sexually explicit.

The whole subject of erotica is a maze. The original authors of erotic literature are often anonymous or pseudonymous. The works themselves frequently appear in several versions, having been pirated, translated, re-translated and bowdlerized by pseudonymous publishers. Today, some important erotica is being re-published by major publishing houses. But much remains in national libraries and institutions which are sometimes ambivalent about the material: it may not be properly catalogued, access can be made difficult and even the basic conservation of books, prints and drawings may be neglected, depending on the attitude of the individual curator. At the same time much erotic art and literature is in the hands of private collectors, some of whom are extremely generous about making rare items available for copying and photography, while others are less so.

Thanks to some pioneer publishing since the Second World War, some parts of this maze of erotica will already be familiar to most readers. This book opens up much more of the maze to the general public – and provides a guide. As a guide, the book makes no claim to being comprehensive or definitive; it is an exploration.

--------- PANDORA'S BOX ---------

Sadly, following the liberalization of the laws governing the publication of sexual material, a great deal of second-rate, ugly and pernicious stuff has also become available. This was inevitable but it does not argue for suppression. Indeed, it makes it vital for good erotica to be published, so that we can see for ourselves the difference between the life-enhancing, and the sordid and destructive. Until sex takes its proper place on our bookshelves, it will be difficult for it to take its proper place in our lives. Women-haters and those addicted to cruelty and violence must look elsewhere – there is nothing in this book for you.

All anthologies involve selection, and the reader needs to know what principles have governed the process. This book is an exploration of mainstream sexuality as revealed in writing and images that were, until comparatively recently, forbidden, banned or privately distributed. For that reason there is little from the second half of the twentieth century, when the cultural climate began to change and the restrictions on writing openly about sex were relaxed. Since the historic obscenity trials of the 1960s (of *Lady Chatterley's Lover* and *Fanny Hill* in the UK and *Tropic of Cancer* in the USA), writers and artists of every type, and every quality, have been able to deal with sex in an increasingly explicit way. There have been regrettable anachronisms (the *Oz* trial in the UK, for example) but in general writers and artists no longer have to look over their shoulders or fear a knock at the door if their chosen subject is sex. This anthology is concerned with the forbidden. Whatever their motives for producing the work, many of the writers and artists included here were pushing out the frontiers and risked penalties ranging from loss of reputation, position and income, to fines, imprisonment or banishment. There are exceptions, and to round off the work there are quotations and illustra-

ABOVE Erotic art is found among the very earliest evidence we have of human culture. This stone figure, popularly known as the Venus of Willendorf, after the place in Austria where it was discovered, was carved in the Paleolithic period around 30,000 BC. Her newly-acquired name is not inappropriate. She is clearly an object of worship: an idealized woman, a celebration of female sexuality and fecundity.

RIGHT Gustav Klimt's drawing of a woman masturbating. It was a subject he had explored before, in 1907, when his exquisite illustrations of Lucian's *Dialogues* were condemned by the authorities. Klimt worked in Vienna, the city of Freud when the pioneer of psychoanalysis was at his most brilliant, yet his own explorations of human sexuality met with hostility. Science was about to unleash the most terrible war in history; in the technological clamour ears were deaf to the voice of Art, eyes blind to the no less important human discoveries which Art can make.
BELOW Another, unknown, artist looks at the auto-erotic.

tions from many other sources, but this is essentially an anthology of what has, in its time, been forbidden by Western culture.

The anthology is predominantly Western but it also contains a good deal of material from the older, wiser civilizations of the East, which have regarded sex as an important (and largely guiltless) subject for thousands of years. In order even to publish these texts in the West – and avoid prosecution – subterfuge was necessary. *Kama Sutra, Ananga-Ranga* and *The Perfumed Garden* were produced and distributed by Sir Richard Burton and others under the auspices of the 'Kama Shastra Society – London and Benares', which was only a blind.

The writers included in this anthology – with a few notable exceptions from all periods and cultures – are men. This is unavoidable, because historically most writers (certainly most writers of erotica) were men. We are pleased to say that this is changing now. But this male bias does not mean that there is nothing here of interest to women. Perhaps it is significant that much of the best erotic writing (*Fanny Hill* or *Satyra Sotadica*, for example) uses the device of the first-person narrative, with a woman as the narrator!

This is not a literary anthology in the normal sense – it is an erotic anthology. The illustrations are just as important as the text, and the extracts which make up the greater part of the text have been selected not primarily for their literary value, but because they have something to tell us about sexuality.

In compiling this anthology we have not so much sorted the sheep from the goats as penned a wide selection of both beasts together in order to make comparisons and enjoy the variety. This involves putting minor writers with the great and the good; the lewd and the bawdy with the sublime and the religious. The illustrations are similarly diverse, ranging from fine and delicate to rude and disgraceful. We are sorry if some of these juxtapositions are surprising. Sex has many aspects.

A GAME FOR FOUR OR MORE PLAYERS

An anthology of this kind is not so much a book as a group encounter. Nobody can leave their sexuality at home: here we all are, writers, researchers, editors, artists, designers and of course you, the reader, all with our own erotic experiences and appetites, our own aesthetic and moral opinions, involved in an extraordinary bring and buy sale. Freud wrote in one of his letters, 'I am accustoming myself to the idea of regarding every sexual act as a process in which four persons are involved. We shall have a lot to discuss about that.' In which case, like one of Cecil B. De Mille's epics, this anthology has a cast of thousands.

This is not a solemn book. It does have a serious subject. Sex is very important and if you are unhappy about it for any reason you should seek advice. If your doctor is unsympathetic (or stupid) ask to be referred to a sex counsellor or look in the telephone book for self-help organizations.

A WORD FROM OUR SPONSOR

Eros, the Greek god of love, gave his name to this 'erotic' anthology. All gods are used to having their names taken in vain, of course – Love more than most – but we would like to get it right. He appears in the book from time to time, often in unlikely places, but do these fleeting glimpses justify the title? We think so. After all, without him it is all nothing but empty shadow-play.

Lay your sleeping head, my love,
Human on my faithless arm;
Time and fevers burn away
Individual beauty from
Thoughtful children, and the grave
Proves the child ephemeral:
But in my arms till break of day
Let the living creature lie,
Mortal, guilty, but to me
The entirely beautiful.

FROM *LULLABY*
W. H. AUDEN

◇

BELOW Eros attending Venus in a painting by an unknown twentieth-century artist.

◇

PART ONE

The moment of desire

The moment of desire! the moment of desire! the virgin
That pines for man shall awaken her womb to enormous joys
In the secret shadows of her chamber: the youth shut up from
The lustful joy shall forget to generate and create an amorous
image
In the shadows of his curtains and in the folds of his silent pillow

FROM *VISIONS OF THE DAUGHTERS OF ALBION*
WILLIAM BLAKE

RIGHT AND OPPOSITE Erotic miniatures from Rajasthan, painted in the Mughal manner. The age-old tradition of Indian miniature painting – which includes a wide diversity of styles – has always involved copying. This means that dating the art can sometimes be a problem, although these paintings are certainly late nineteenth- or early twentieth-century.

How fortunate to have been a young man or woman reaching sexual maturity in India 2,000 years ago! Sex was guiltless, openly discussed, and the sage Vatsyayana had just completed his *Kama Sutra*. This great work collated all the sexual wisdom of previous centuries and presented it as an easily understood guide. Vatsyayana wrote the book in his later years as a religious duty: his intention was to enable young people to avoid the shocks and pitfalls of sex and to enjoy its wonders. Included was guidance on every aspect of the relationship between men and women, together with a no-nonsense manual of sexual instruction covering everything from biting and scratching to fellatio and love-making postures. This extract gives the flavour of the work.

When a woman sees her lover is fatigued by constant congress, without having his desire satisfied, she should, with his permission, lay him down upon his back, and give him assistance by acting his part. She may also do this to satisfy the curiosity of her lover, or her own desire of novelty.

There are two ways of doing this, the first is when during

congress she turns round, and gets on the top of her lover, in such a manner as to continue the congress, without obstructing the pleasure of it; and the other is when she acts the man's part from the beginning. At such a time, with flowers in her hair hanging loose, and her smiles broken by hard breathings, she should press upon her lover's bosom with her own breasts, and lowering her head frequently, should do in return the same actions which he used to do before, returning his blows and chaffing him, should say, 'I was laid down by you, and fatigued with hard congress, I shall now therefore lay you down in return.' She should then again manifest her own bashfulness, her fatigue, and her desire of stopping the congress.

Earlier in the *Kama Sutra* Vatsyayana explains the importance of wooing and foreplay to young men:

Women, being of a tender nature, want tender beginnings, and when they are forcibly approached by men with whom they are but slightly acquainted, they sometimes suddenly become haters of sexual connection, and sometimes even haters of the male sex.

A gust of wind will blow open the petals of a poppy that is slow in blossoming. Love suddenly brings the spirit of a girl to flower.

FROM THE SANSCRIT
AMARU, c. 800 AD

Nearly 2,000 years after the *Kama Sutra* was written – at a time when India was the 'jewel in the crown' of the British Empire, but its ancient wisdom largely ignored – the young Frank Harris was receiving his sex education in the usual Western manner.

A week later Strangways astonished us both by telling how he had made up to the nursemaid of his younger sisters and got into her bed at night. The first time she wouldn't let him do anything, it appeared, but, after a night or two, he managed to touch her sex and assured us it was all covered with silky hairs. A little later he told us how she had locked her door and how the next day he had taken off the lock and got into bed with her again. At first she was cross, or pretended to be, he said, but he kept on kissing and begging her, and bit by bit she yielded, and he touched her sex again. 'It was a slit,' he said. A few nights later, he told us he had put his prick into her and, 'Oh! by gum, it was wonderful, wonderful!'

'But how did you do it?' we wanted to know, and he gave us his whole experience.

'Girls love kissing,' he said, 'and so I kissed and kissed her and put my leg on her, and her hand on my cock and I kept touching her breasts and her cunny (that's what she calls it) and at last I got on her between her legs and she guided my prick into her cunt (God, it was wonderful!) and now I go with her every night and often in the day as well. She likes her cunt touched, but very gently,' he added; 'she showed me how to do it with one finger like this,' and he suited the action to the word.

Strangways in a moment became to us not only a hero but a miracle-man; we pretended not to believe him in order to make him tell us the truth and we were almost crazy with breathless desire.

I got him to invite me up to the vicarage and I saw Mary the nurse-girl there, and she seemed to me almost a woman and spoke to him as 'Master Will' and he kissed her, though she frowned and said, 'Leave off' and 'Behave yourself,' very angrily; but I felt that her anger was put on to prevent my guessing the truth. I was aflame with desire and when I told Howard, he, too, burned with lust, and took me out for a walk and questioned me all over again, and under a haystack in the country we gave ourselves to a bout of frigging, which for the first time thrilled me with pleasure.

All the time we were playing with ourselves, I kept

thinking of Mary's hot slit, as Strangways had described it, and, at length, a real orgasm came and shook me; the imagining had intensified my delight.

Nothing in my life up to that moment was comparable in joy to that story of sexual pleasure as described, and acted for us, by Strangways.

Frank Harris published the first volume of *My Life and Loves* in 1922, when he was sixty-eight and 'half-drowned in the brackish flood of old age'. He wanted it to be the most honest autobiography ever written. It would record his contacts with the important people of his time (and he had indeed met most of them), but it would also be truthful about sex. In the foreword he wrote: 'Nine men and women out of ten go through life without realizing their own special nature: they cannot lose their souls, for they have never found them. That's why I love this book in spite of all its shortcomings and all its faults . . .'. Unfortunately, the book marked his downfall. The world was not ready for 'Frank-ness' of this sort.

Frank Harris was a curious amalgam. He was one of the greatest editors of his time (notably of the *Saturday Review*), the staunch friend and biographer of Oscar Wilde who dedicated *An Ideal Husband* to him, a lifelong romantic and fierce radical. He was a notorious seducer but genuinely loved women for themselves. When those men he had offended had their revenge after the publication of *My Life and Loves* it was for radical onslaughts like this one against the Anglo-Saxon male: 'He has made of his wife a meek upper servant or slave . . . who has hardly any intellectual interests and whose spiritual being only finds a narrow outlet in her mother instincts!'

George Bernard Shaw, a friend for more than forty years, wrote of Harris: 'He blazed through London like a comet, leaving a trail of deeply annoyed persons behind him, and like a meteor through America . . . I think I know pretty well all the grievances his detractors had against him; but if I had to write his epitaph it should run "Here lies a man of letters who hated cruelty and injustice and bad art, and never spared them in his own interest. RIP."'

We shall hear Frank's voice (a remarkable *basso profundo* which one of his mistresses confessed 'made her sex open and shut' whenever she heard it) from time to time in this anthology. He recalled his own first sexual encounter with clarity.

Before every church festival there was a good deal of practice with the organist, and girls from neighboring houses joined in our classes. One girl alone sang alto and she and I were separated from the other boys and girls; the upright piano was put across the corner of the room and we two sat or stood behind it, almost out of sight of all the other singers, the organist, of course, being seated in front of the piano. The girl E. . . . , who sang alto with me, was about my own age; she was very pretty, or seemed so to me, with golden hair and blue eyes, and I always made up to

OPPOSITE, ABOVE AND BELOW The artist who produced these fine charcoal drawings was obliged to remain anonymous, signing his work 'A1'. They were taken from the series entitled 'Claire Obscure' first published in Vienna in 1935. These are skilful confections: suggestive shadows from which naked flesh shines like an erotic beacon.

During the endless sunset of the Austro-Hungarian Empire, its splendidly decadent capital, Vienna, produced a wealth of erotic art. When A1's wanton (ABOVE) first enjoyed the attention of her young lover in 1935, her painted bronze sister (OPPOSITE) had already had her skirt lifted by inquisitive fingers for nearly 40 years.

her as well as I could, in my boyish way. One day while the organist was explaining something, E. . . . stood up on the chair and leant over the back of the piano to hear better or see more. Seated in my chair behind her, I caught sight of her legs, for her dress rucked up behind as she leaned over; at once my breath stuck in my throat. Her legs were lovely, I thought, and the temptation came to touch them; for no one could see.

I got up immediately and stood by the chair she was standing on. Casually I let my hand fall against her left leg. She didn't draw her leg away or seem to feel my hand, so I touched her more boldly. She never moved, though now I knew she must have felt my hand. I began to slide my hand up her leg and suddenly my fingers felt the warm flesh on her thigh where the stocking ended above the knee. The feel of her warm flesh made me literally choke with emotion: my hand went on up, warmer and warmer, when suddenly I touched her sex; there was soft down on it. The heart-pulse throbbed in my throat. I have no words to describe the intensity of my sensations.

Thank God, E. . . . did not move or show any sign of distaste. Curiosity was stronger even than desire in me and I felt her sex all over, and at once the idea came into my head that it was like a fig (the Italians, I learned later, called it familiarly *fica*); it opened at my touches and I inserted my finger gently, as Strangways had told me that Mary had taught him to do; still E. . . . did not move. Gently I rubbed the front part of her sex with my finger. I could have kissed her a thousand times out of gratitude.

Suddenly, as I went on, I felt her move, and then again; plainly she was showing me where my touch gave her most pleasure: I could have died for her in thanks; again she moved and I could feel a little mound or small button of flesh right in the front of her sex, above the junction of the inner lips; of course it was her clitoris. I had forgotten all the old Methodist doctor's books till that moment; this fragment of long forgotten knowledge came back to me: gently I rubbed the clitoris and at once she pressed down on my finger for a moment or two. I tried to insert my finger into the vagina; but she drew away at once and quickly, closing her sex as if hurt, so I went back to caressing her tickler.

Suddenly the miracle ceased. The cursed organist had finished his explanation of the new plain chant, and as he touched the first notes on the piano, E. . . . drew her legs together; I took away my hand and she stepped down from the chair. 'You darling, darling,' I whispered, but she frowned, and then just gave me a smile out of the corner of her eye to show me she was not displeased.

Ah, how lovely, how seductive she seemed to me now, a thousand times lovelier and more desirable than ever before. As we stood up to sing again, I whispered to her: 'I love you, love you, dear, dear!'

I can never express the passion of gratitude I felt to her for her goodness, her sweetness in letting me touch her sex. E. . . . it was who opened the Gates of Paradise to me and let me first taste the hidden mysteries of sexual delight. Still after more than fifty years I feel the thrill of the joy she gave me by her response, and

the passionate reverence of my gratitude is still alive in me.

This experience with E. . . . had the most important and unlooked for results. The mere fact that girls could feel sex-pleasure 'just as boys do' increased my liking for them and lifted the whole sexual intercourse to a higher plane in my thought. The excitement and pleasure were so much more intense than anything I had experienced before that I resolved to keep myself for this higher joy. No more self-abuse for me; I knew something infinitely better. One kiss was better, one touch of a girl's sex.

Young Frank's second attempt at seduction, this time with his French tutor, is less successful.

This afternoon Lucille was seated, leaning back in an armchair right in front of the door, for the day was sultry-close, and when Edwards went, I threw myself on the doorstep at her feet: her dress clung to her form, revealing the outlines of her thighs and breasts seductively. I was wild with excitement. Suddenly I noticed her legs were apart; I could see her slim ankles. Pulses awoke throbbing in my forehead and throat: I begged for a kiss and got on my knees to take it: she gave me one; but when I persisted, she repulsed me, saying:

'*Non, non! Sois sage!*' ['No, no! Behave!']

As I returned to my seat reluctantly, the thought came, 'Put your hand up her clothes'; I felt sure I could reach her sex. She was seated on the edge of the chair and leaning back. The mere idea shook and scared me; but what can she do, I thought: she can only get angry. I thought again of all possible consequences: the example with E. . . . came to encourage and hearten me. I leaned round and knelt in front of her, smiling, begging for a kiss, and as she smiled in return, I put my hand boldly right up her clothes on her sex. I felt the soft hairs and the form of it in breathless ecstasy; but I scarcely held it when she sprang upright. 'How dare you?' she cried, trying to push my hand away.

My sensations were too overpowering for words or act; my life was in my fingers; I held her cunt. A moment later I tried to touch her gently with my middle finger as I had touched E. . . . : 'Twas a mistake: I no longer held her sex and at once Lucille whirled round and was free.

'I have a good mind to strike you,' she cried. 'I'll tell Mrs. Edwards,' she snorted indignantly. 'You're a bad, bad boy and I thought you nice. I'll never be kind to you again: I hate you!' She fairly stamped with anger.

I went to her, my whole being one prayer. 'Don't spoil it all,' I cried. 'You hurt so when you are angry, dear.'

She turned to me hotly. 'I'm really angry, angry,' she panted, 'and you're a hateful rude boy and I don't like you any more,' and she turned away again, shaking her dress straight. 'Oh, how could I help it?' I began. 'You're so pretty, oh, you are wonderful, Lucille!'

'Wonderful,' she repeated, sniffing disdainfully, but I saw she was mollified.

'Kiss me,' I pleaded, 'and don't be cross.'

ABOVE An oil painting on canvas atttributed to Lovis Corinth (1858–1925). The painting's subtly pervasive eroticism comes from the woman's expression: we admire the breasts, the long flank – but always seek the face again. It is the whole woman who is erotic.

'I'll never kiss you again,' she replied quickly; 'you can be sure of that.' I went on begging, praising, pleading for ever so long, till at length she took my head in her hands, saying:

'If you'll promise never to do that again, never, I'll give you a kiss and try to forgive you.'

'I can't promise,' I said, 'it was too sweet; but kiss me and I'll try to be good.'

She kissed me a quick peck and pushed me away.

'Didn't you like it?' I whispered, 'I did awfully. I can't tell you how I thrilled: oh, thank you, Lucille, thank you, you are the sweetest girl in the world, and I shall always be grateful to you, you dear!'

She looked down at me musingly, thoughtfully; I felt I was gaining ground.

'You are lovely there,' I ventured in a whisper. 'Please dear, what do you call it? I saw *chat* once: is that right, "pussy?"'

'Don't talk of it,' she cried impatiently. 'I hate to think –'

'Be kind, Lucille,' I pleaded. 'You'll never be the same to me again: you were pretty before, chic and provoking, but now you're sacred. I don't love you, I adore you, reverence you, darling! May I say "pussy?"'

'You're a strange boy,' she said at length, 'but you must never do that again; it's nasty and I don't like it. I –'

'Don't say such things!' I cried, pretending indignation. 'You don't know what you're saying – nasty! Look, I'll kiss the fingers that have touched your pussy,' and I suited the action to the word.

'Oh, don't,' she cried and caught my hand in hers, 'don't!' But somehow she leaned against me at the same time and left her lips on mine. Bit by bit my right hand went down to her sex again, this time on the outside of her dress, but at once she tore herself away and would not let me come near her again. My insane desire had again made me blunder.

———————◊———————

Henry Miller's attitude towards sexuality and women is very different from Frank Harris's – he does not romanticize the one and idealize the other. On the contrary, he goes out of his way to strip away pretensions and to shock in doing so, but (only in his best writing) goes on to show you a new beauty in what remains. It is not 'reality' any more than Frank Harris's writing is – they both involve literary artifice – but it is a fundamental difference in attitude and approach. There are extracts from his best work later in the anthology. The fire and poetry of *Tropic of Cancer* and *Tropic of Capricorn* were never again achieved, but the later writing has its memorable incidents. This account of Miller's early sexual explorations from *Plexus* would be a bleak little episode were it not for the strangely touching impulse of the girl Kitty at the end.

One day George drew me aside to tell me something confidential . . . There was a young country girl he wanted me to meet. We

may i feel said he
(i'll squeal said she
just once said he)
it's fun said she

(may i touch said he
how much said she
a lot said he)
why not said she

(let's go said he
not too far said she
what's too far said he
where you are said she)

may i stay said he
(which way said she
like this said he
if you kiss said she

may i move said he
is it love said she)
if you're willing said he
(but you're killing said she

but it's life said he
but your wife said she
now said he)
ow said she

(tiptop said he
don't stop said she
oh no said he)
go slow said she

(cccome?said he
ummm said she)
you're divine!said he
(you are Mine said she)

E. E. CUMMINGS (1894–1962)

ABOVE A watercolour on paper by 'Fay D', a Hungarian artist working in Paris in the 1920s. The bronze reliefs (OPPOSITE) are from the same period but were produced in Germany.

could find her down near the bridge, toward dark, with the right signal.

'She looks twenty, though she's only a kid,' said George, as we hastened toward the spot. 'A virgin, of course, but a dirty little devil. You can't get much more than a good feel, Hen. I've tried everything, but it's no go.'

Kitty was her name. It suited her. A plain-looking girl, but full of sap and curiosity. Hump for the monkeys.

'Hello,' says George, as we sidle up to her. 'How's tricks? Want you to meet a friend of mine, from the city.'

Her hand was tingling with warmth and desire. It seemed to me she was blushing, but it may have been simply the abundant health which was bursting through her cheeks.

'Give him a hug and squeeze.'

Kitty flung her arms about me and pressed her warm body tight to mine. In a moment her tongue was down my throat. She bit my lips, my ear lobes, my neck. I put my hand under her skirt and through the slit in her flannel drawers. No protest. She began to groan and murmur. Finally she had an orgasm.

'How was it, Hen? What did I tell you?'

We chatted a while to give Kitty a breathing spell, then George locked horns with her. It was cold and wet under the bridge, but the three of us were on fire. Again George tried to get it in, but Kitty managed to wriggle away.

The most he could do was to put it between her legs, where she held it like a vise.

As we were walking back toward the road Kitty asked if she couldn't visit us sometime – when we got back to the city. She had never been to New York.

'Sure,' said George, 'let Herbie bring you. He knows his way around.'

'But I won't have any money,' said Kitty.

'Don't worry about that,' said big-hearted George, 'we'll take care of you.'

'Do you think your mother would trust you?' I asked.

Kitty replied that her mother didn't give a damn what she did. 'It's the old man: he tries to work me to the bone.'

'Never mind,' said George, 'leave it to me.'

You were ashamed
of the soft down on your bottom,
I of my member's
huge-bulbed gracelessness:
delicately I caressed
that delicate bottom;
graciously you rewarded
gracelessness.

Never were two more suited,
each one's shame
answered with, first, affection,
then desire:
now I lie sleepless
dwelling on your shame,
and shamelessly desiring
your desire.

BECAUSE OF LOVE
ROBIN SKELTON (1925–   )

In parting she lifted her dress, of her own accord, and invited us to give her a last good feel.

'Maybe I won't be so shy,' she said, 'when I get to the city.'

Then, impulsively, she reached into our flies, took out our cocks, and kissed them – almost reverently. 'I'll dream about you tonight,' she whispered. She was almost on the point of tears.

For reality in sexual autobiography – plainly expressed and stripped of charm – there is no more remarkable book than *My Secret Life*, written by the unknown Victorian Englishman who called himself 'Walter'. Printed privately in eleven volumes – of which only six complete sets have been traced – it is one of the most extraordinary social documents from that period. The author diarizes, in obsessive detail, each of his sexual encounters (more than 1,500) from youth to late middle age, a period spanning most of the Victorian era. The style is often awkward and

BELOW This astonishing watercolour is from a series of 33 produced by an anonymous Czech artist at the turn of the century.

crude, some of the incidents cruel and exploitative (nothing compared with, for example, the violent and sadistic passages which feature in the fashionable erotica of Anaïs Nin, but that is fantasy) yet *My Secret Life* has the unmistakable ring of truth about it. In this early episode in an eventful sex life Walter completes his seduction of his mother's maid, Charlotte. On her day off they go to an 'accommodation house'.

It was a gentleman's house, although the room cost but five shillings: red curtains, looking-glasses, wax lights, clean linen, a huge chair, a large bed, and a cheval-glass, large enough for the biggest couple to be reflected in, were all there. I examined all with the greatest curiosity, but my curiosity was greater for other things; of all the delicious, voluptuous recollections, that day stands among the brightest; for the first time in my life I saw all a woman's charms, and exposed my own manhood to one; both of us knew but little of the opposite sex. With difficulty I got her to undress to her chemise, then with but my shirt on, how I revelled in her nakedness, feeling from her neck to her ankles, lingering with my fingers in every crack and cranny of her body; from armpits to cunt, all was new to me. With what fierce eyes, after modest struggles, and objections to prevent, and I had forced open her reluctant thighs, did I gloat on her cunt; wondering at its hairy outer covering and lips, its red inner flaps, at the hole so closed up, and so much lower down and hidden than I thought it to be; soon, at its look and feel, impatience got the better of me; hurriedly I covered it with my body and shed my sperm in it. Then with what curiosity I paddled my finger in it afterwards, again to stiffen, thrust, wriggle, and spend. All this I recollect as if it occurred but yesterday, I shall recollect it to the last day of my life, for it was a honey-moon of novelty; years afterwards I often thought of it when fucking other women.

We fell asleep, and must have been in the room some hours, when we awakened about three o'clock. We had eaten nothing that day, and both were hungry, she objected to wash before me, or to piddle; how charming it was to overcome that needless modesty, what a treat to me to see that simple operation. We dressed and left, went to a quietish public-house, and had some simple food and beer, which set me up, I was ready to do all over again, and so was she. We went back to the house and again to bed; the woman smiled when she saw us; the feeling, looking, titillating, baudy inciting, and kissing recommenced. With what pleasure she felt and handled my prick, nor did she make objection to my investigations into her privates, though saying she would not let me. Her thighs opened, showing the red-lipped, hairy slit; I kissed it, she kissed my cock, nature taught us both what to do. Again we fucked, I found it a longish operation, and when I tried later again, was surprised to find that it would not stiffen for more than a minute, and an insertion failed. I found out that day that there were limits to my powers. Both tired out, our day's pleasure over, we rose and took a hackney coach towards home.

ABOVE One of a series of engravings for 'Les Diaboliques' by the French artist Leon Richet.

E xploration of another, and the novelty of doing so for the first time, is of course one of the wonders of sex. But there are pitfalls for the inexperienced, and all too often in our culture the young have been left groping – both literally and metaphorically – in the dark. In the West, until comparatively recently, there was no proper information available on sex even for adults. Armed with tales from their peers, which were frequently full of absurd notions, and driven only by instinct, the young were pitched straight into the practical with little or no theoretical knowledge – often with tragic results. In matters of sex education, the Dark Ages continued until well into the twentieth century in

BELOW AND OPPOSITE All three works are by the Japanese master of the coloured woodcut Utamaro Utagawa (1753–1806). *The Song of the Pillow* is considered by many to be his masterpiece.

the West. In eighth-century Japan – while Europe was still enjoying all other aspects of the Dark Ages – well produced sexual textbooks and manuals, and elegant erotic novels, were already widely available. There was also a translation of a third-century Chinese medical text book, the *Pao P'u Tzu*, dealing with sex. Only towards the end of the nineteenth century was anything comparable published in the West. Nor was Havelock Ellis's monumental and long overdue *Studies in the Psychology of Sex* greeted with enthusiasm by Victorian society, worthy and well-intentioned though it was. In Japan, the idea of sex education is not only time-honoured, it is a concept enshrined in the country's creation myths. Who could find any-

I moan for love
Before my birds.
They also are in a cage.

GEISHA SONG
ANONYMOUS

In a soft box of plushy fluff,
Black, but with glints of copper-red
And edges crinkly like a ruff,
Lies the great god of gems in bed.

Throbbing with sap and life, and sends
In wafts the best news ever sent,
A perfume his ecstatic friends
Think stolen from each element.

But contemplate this temple, cont-
emplate, then get your breath, and kiss
The jewel having fits in front,
The ruby grinning for its bliss,

Flowers of the inner court, kid brother
So mad about the taller one
It kisses till they both hay-smother
And puff, then pulse, in unison. . . .

FROM *ANOINTED VESSEL*
PAUL VERLAINE (1844–96)

ABOVE One of a series of highly
mannered erotic illustrations
drawn by the Viennese artist
Joseph Ortloff in 1922.

thing objectionable or unseemly in sex education when every child is taught that Japan's mythical founders, Izanami and Izanaji, received instruction in lovemaking from two shepherdesses?

Given the thinness of the paper walls in traditional Japanese houses it is just as well that children learned about sex before having to draw their own conclusions. The childish interpretation of the sexual act is generally to regard it as a violent attack on the mother by the father. This trauma has been used by Freudians to explain behavioural problems in some adults, notably the more morbid obsessions of poor, tormented Edgar Allan Poe who spent his formative years in the close confines of theatrical lodgings with his parents. Mercifully, Japan has been spared a succession of Edgar Allan Poes, although its literature is not without its violence and morbidity.

Lovers overlooked, voyeuristically, is a common theme in *shunga* – the erotic prints of Japan. The same motif is popular in Western erotica, often presented as a 'first lesson in love'.

———◊———

Although watching others making love may be genuinely instructive, in erotic literature, such episodes are generally confections designed to titillate. This lively example comes from the *Voluptuous Confessions of a French Lady of Fashion*, published in the beautifully-produced Victorian underground magazine *The Boudoir*. The heroine is watching her young aunt with her fiancé from a hiding place in the grounds of her grandmother's estate.

I applied my eye, as I held my breath, and was witness of what I am going to relate.

Bertha, hanging on the neck of Monsieur B., devoured him with kisses.

'Come,' she said, 'my darling, I was very unhappy to refuse you, but I was afraid. Here, at least, I am assured. This beautiful Mimi, what pleasure I am going to give him. Hold, I come already in thinking of it! But how shall we place ourselves?'

'All right; but first let me see again my dear Bibi, it is such a long time I have wanted her.'

You may guess what my thoughts were at this moment. But what were they going to do? I was not left long in suspense.

Monsieur B., going down on one knee, raised the skirts of Bertha. What charms he exposed! Under that fine cambric chemise were legs worthy of Venus, encased in silk stockings, secured above the knee by garters of the colour of fire; then two adorable thighs, white, round, and firm, which rejoined above, surmounted by a fleece of black and lustrous curls, the abundance and length of which were a great surprise to me, compared above all to the light chestnut moss which commenced to cover the same part in myself.

'How I love it,' said Alfred. 'How beautiful and fresh it is! Open yourself a little, my angel, that I may kiss those adorable lips!'

Bertha did as he demanded; her thighs, in opening, made me

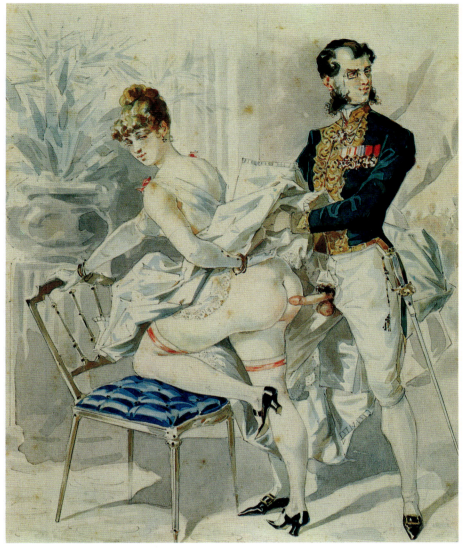

LEFT A gently satirical watercolour
by the nineteenth-century Belgian
artist Louis Morin.

see a rosy slit, upon which her lover glued his lips. Bertha seemed
in ecstasy! Shutting her eyes, and speaking broken words; making a forward movement in response to this curious caress, which
transported her so.

'Ah, you kill me . . . encore! . . . go on! It's coming . . . I . . . I
. . . I'm coming! . . . Ah, ah!'

What was she doing? Good God! I had never supposed that any
pleasure pertained to that part. Yet, however, I began to feel
myself in the same spot some particular titillations, which made
me understand it.

Alfred got up, supporting Bertha, who appeared to have lost all
strength; but she soon recovered herself, and embraced him with
ardour.

'Come, now, let me put him in,' she said. 'But how are we
going to do it?'

'Turn yourself, my dear, and incline over this unworthy seat; let
me do it.'

Then, to my great surprise, Bertha, by rapid and excited movement, herself undid the trousers of Alfred, and lifting his shirt above his navel she exposed to my view such an extraordinary object, that I was almost surprised into a scream. What could be this unknown member, the head of which was so rosy and exalted, its length and thickness giving me a vertigo?

Bertha evidently did not share my fears, for she took this frightful instrument in her hand, caressed it a moment, and said: 'Let us begin, Monsieur Mimi, come into your little companion, and be sure not to go away too soon.'

She lifted up her clothes behind and exposed to the light of day two globes of dazzling whiteness, separated by a crack of which I could only see a slight trace; she then inclined herself, and, placing her hands on the wooden seat, presented her adorable bottom to her lover.

Alfred just behind her took his enormous instrument in hand, and wetting it with a little saliva commenced to introduce it

RIGHT Louis Morin was born in Brussels in 1851. The eroticism in his work is usually lightened by humour, as in this wonderfully idealized naval engagement.

between the two lips which I had perceived. Bertha did not flinch, and opened as much as possible the part which she presented, which seemed to open itself, and at length absorbed this long and thick machine, which appeared monstrous to me; however, it penetrated so well that it disappeared entirely, and the belly of its happy possessor came to be glued to the buttocks of my aunt.

There was then a conjunction of combined movements, followed by broken words – 'Ah! . . . I feel him . . . He is getting into me,' said Bertha. 'Push it all well into me . . . softly . . . let me come first. Ah! . . . I feel it . . . I'm coming! . . . Quicker! I come . . . stop . . . there you are! I die . . . I . . . I . . . Ah!'

As to Alfred, his eyes half closed, his hands holding the hips of my aunt, he seemed inexpressibly happy.

'Hold,' said he, 'my angel, my all, ah! How fine it is! Push well! Do come . . . there; it's coming, is it not! Go on . . . go on . . . I feel you're coming . . . push well, my darling!'

Both stopped a moment; my aunt appeared exhausted; but did not change her position; at length she lightly turned her head to give her lover a kiss, saying – 'Now, both together! You let me know when you are ready.'

The scene recommenced. At the end of some instants, Alfred, in turn, cried out – 'Ah! . . . I feel it coming . . . are you ready, my love? Yes . . . yes . . . there I am . . . push, again . . . go on . . . I spend . . . I am yours. I . . . I . . . Ah! What a pleasure . . . I . . . sp— . . . I spend!'

A long silence followed; Alfred seemed to have lost his strength, and ready to fall over Bertha, who was obliged to put her arms straight to bear him. Alfred recovered himself, and I again saw that marvellous instrument coming out of the crack, where he had been so well treated. But how changed he was. His size diminished to half, red and damp, and I saw something like a white and viscous pearl come from it and drop to the floor.

Alfred began to put his clothes in order; during which my aunt, who had got up, put her arms round the neck of her lover, and covered him with kisses.

What had I been doing during this time? My imagination, excited to the highest degree, made me repeat one part of the pleasures which transported my actors.

At the critical moment I lifted petticoat and chemise, and my inexperienced hand contented itself by exploring that tender part. I thus assured myself that I was made the same as Bertha, but I knew not yet what use or consolation that hand could give. This very morning was to enlighten me.

After plenty of kissing, Bertha said to Monsieur B. – 'Listen, my dear, I have been thinking. You know that my apartment is quite isolated; without my *femme de chambre*, who sleeps in the ante-room, no one could know of our rendezvous, and we could pass some adorable nights together.

'Under a pretext of wanting something for my toilette, I will send Julie to Paris to-morrow afternoon, and after the evening we can join each other. Be on the look out, you can give me a sign during the day of the hour when you can slip away to me. I beg you to take the most minute precautions.'

And all her face was honey to my
mouth,
And all her body pasture to mine eyes;
The long lithe arms and hotter hands
than fire,
The quivering flanks, hair smelling of
the south,
The bright light feet, the splendid
supple thighs
And glittering eyelids of my soul's
desire.

FROM *LOVE AND SLEEP*
ALGERNON CHARLES SWINBURNE
(1837–1909)

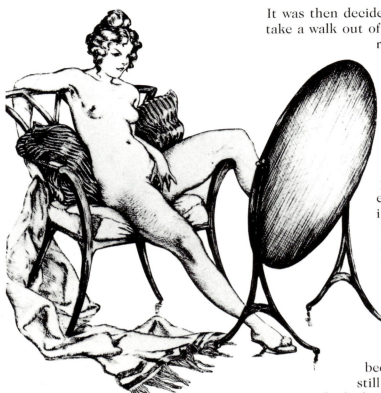

It was then decided that Monsieur B. should go first. He was to take a walk out of the park, and during the time my aunt would regain her room by the private staircase. Monsieur B. went out, and I remained hidden in my brambles till he was sufficiently far off not to have any fear of being perceived by him. Observing that my aunt had not yet come out, I stopped and looked again. There was in the pavilion a chamber pot and wash basin; I saw Bertha fill the latter, lift up her petticoats, and stoop over it. She was placed right in front of me, and nothing could escape my view. As she did this her slit opened, it seemed to me a much more lively carnation, the interior and the edges, even up to the fleecy mound which surrounded it, seemed inundated with the same liquor which I had seen come from Monsieur B.

Bertha commenced an ample ablution, and I was going away from my place as softly as possible when I remained fixed, glued to the spot. The hand of my aunt, refreshed with care all the parts which had been so well worked. All at once I saw her stop still, then a finger fixed upon a little eminence which showed itself prominently; this finger rubbed lightly at first, then with a kind of fury. At length Bertha gave the same symptoms of pleasure which I had often seen before.

I had seen enough of it! I understood it all! I retired and made haste to take a long tortuous path, which brought me to the chateau. My head was on fire, my bosom palpitated, and my steps tottered, but I was determined at once to play by myself the last act I had seen, and which required no partner.

I arrived in my room in a state of madness, threw my hat on the floor, shut and double locked the door, and put myself on the bed. I turned up my clothes to the waist, and, recollecting to the minutest details what Bertha had done with her hand, I placed mine between my legs. Some essays were at first fruitless, but I found at length the point I searched for. The rest was easy; I had too well observed to deceive myself. A delicious sensation seized me; I continued with fury, and soon fell into such an ecstasy that I lost consciousness.

When I came to myself I was in the same position, my hand all moistened by an unknown dew.

I sat up quite confused, and it was a long time before I entirely came to myself. It was nearly the hour of *déjeuner*, so I made haste to dress and went down.

My aunt was already in the salon with my grandmother. I looked at her on entering; she was beautiful and fresh, her colour in repose, her eyes brilliant, so that one would have sworn she had just risen from an excellent morning's sleep, her toilette, in exquisite and simple taste, set off her charming figure. As to me I cast down my eyes and felt myself blush.

ABOVE A drawing by Joseph Ortloff; the auto-erotic possibilities of mirrors are a recurring motif in erotic art.

The extract from *The Boudoir* owes something to the most influential, and arguably the best, erotic novel in the English language, John Cleland's *Fanny Hill*, more properly entitled *Memoirs of a Woman of Pleasure*. A century and a half before Bertha is overlooked by her inquisitive niece, the young Fanny Hill is allowed to witness an amorous encounter as part of her education as a whore.

At five in the evening, next day, Phoebe, punctual to her promise, came to me as I sat alone in my own room, and beckon'd me to follow her.

We went down the back-stairs very softly, and opening the door of a dark closet, where there was some old furniture kept, and some cases of liquor, she drew me in after her, and fastening the door upon us, we had no light but what came through a long crevice in the partition between ours and the light closet, where the scene of action lay; so that sitting on those low cases, we could, with the greatest ease, as well as clearness, see all objects (ourselves unseen), only by applying our eyes close to the crevice, where the moulding of a panel had warped, or started a little on the other side.

BELOW Nineteenth-century publishers of erotica were quick to exploit each new technical advance. This superb anonymous engraving was produced in 1892 by the process then known as heliogravure (photogravure).

The young gentleman was the first person I saw, with his back directly towards me, looking at a print. Polly was not yet come: in less than a minute tho', the door opened, and she came in; and at the noise the door made he turned about, and came to meet her, with an air of the greatest tenderness and satisfaction.

After saluting her, he led her to a couch that fronted us, where they both sat down, and the young Genoese help'd her to a glass of wine, with some Naples biscuit on a salver.

Presently, when they had exchanged a few kisses, and questions in broken English on one side, he began to unbutton, and, in fine, stript to his shirt.

As if this had been the signal agreed on for pulling off all their clothes, a scheme which the heat of the season perfectly favoured, Polly began to draw her pins, and as she had no stays to unlace, she was in a trice, with her gallant's officious assistance, undress'd to all but her shift.

When he saw this, his breeches were immediately loosen'd, waist and knee bands, and slipped over his ankles, clean off; his shirt collar was unbuttoned too: then, first giving Polly an

ABOVE An engraving by an unknown artist, probably Antoine Borel, c. 1780.
RIGHT A Russian snuff box made in about 1830.

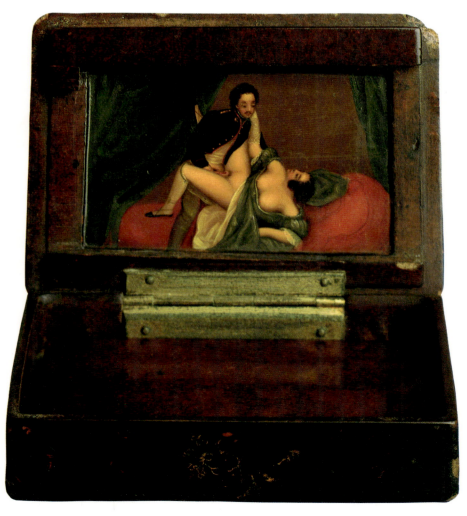

encouraging kiss, he stole, as it were, the shift off the girl, who being, I suppose, broke and familiariz'd to this humour, blush'd indeed, but less than I did at the apparition of her, now standing stark-naked, just as she came out of the hands of pure nature, with her black hair loose and afloat down her dazzling white neck and shoulders, whilst the deepen'd carnation of her cheeks went off gradually into the hue of glaz'd snow: for such were the bland-ed tints and polish of her skin.

This girl could not be above eighteen: her face regular and sweet-featur'd, her shape exquisite; nor could I help envying her two ripe enchanting breasts, finely plump'd out in flesh, but with-al so round, so firm, that they sustain'd themselves, in scorn of any stay: then their nipples, pointing different ways, mark'd their pleasing separation; beneath them lay the delicious tract of the belly, which terminated in a parting or rift scarce discernible, that modestly seem'd to retire downwards, and seek shelter between two plump fleshy thighs: the curling hair that over-spread its delightful front, clothed it with the richest sable fur in the universe: in short, she was evidently a subject for the painter to court her sitting to them for a pattern of female beauty, in all the true pride and pomp of nakedness.

The young Italian (still in his shirt) stood gazing and trans-ported at the sight of beauties that might have fir'd a dying her-mit; his eager eyes devour'd her, as she shifted attitudes at his discretion: neither were his hands excluded their share of the high feast, but wander'd, on the hunt of pleasure, over every part and inch of her body, so qualified to afford the most exquisite sense of it.

In the meantime, one could not help observing the swell of his shirt before, that bolster'd out, and shewed the condition of things behind the curtain: but he soon remov'd it, by slipping his shirt over his head; and now, as to nakedness, they had nothing to reproach one another.

The young gentleman, by Phoebe's guess, was about two and twenty; tall and well limb'd. His body was finely form'd, and of a most vigorous make, square-shoulder'd, and broad-chested: his face was not remarkable in any way, but for a nose inclining to the Roman, eyes large, black, and sparkling, and a ruddiness in his cheeks that was the more a grace, for his complexion was of the brownest, not of that dusky dun colour which excludes the idea of freshness, but of that clear, olive gloss, which, glowing with life, dazzles perhaps less than fairness, and yet pleases more, when it pleases at all. His hair, being too short to tie, fell no lower than his neck, in short easy curls; and he had a few sprigs about his paps, that garnish'd his chest in a style of strength and manliness. Then his grand movement, which seem'd to rise out of a thicket of curling hair that spread from the root all round thighs and belly up to the navel, stood stiff and upright, but of a size to frighten me, by sympathy, for the small tender part which was the object of its fury, and which now lay expos'd to my fairest view; for he had, immediately on stripping off his shirt, gently push'd her down on the couch, which stood conveniently to break her willing fall. Her thighs were spread out to their utmost exten-

ABOVE Erotic pillboxes became popular in the eighteenth century, often with ladies. This pair is French.

ABOVE AND BELOW Scenes from
Thérèse philosophe, first published
in 1748, and illustrated through
its numerous editions by the best
engravers of the day, including
Delcroche (in 1780) and Binet (in
1782). In creating *Fanny Hill*
(more properly *Memoirs of a
Woman of Pleasure*, also first
published in 1748) John Cleland
was able to draw upon a long
tradition of French libertine
literature.

sion, and discovered between them the mark of the sex, the red-
centred cleft of flesh, whose lips, vermilioning inwards, exprest a
small ruby line in sweet miniature, such as *Guido's* touch or
colouring could never attain to the life or delicacy of.

Phoebe, at this, gave me a gentle jog, to prepare me for a whispered question: whether I thought my little maiden-head was
much less? But my attention was too much engross'd, too much
enwrapp'd with all I saw, to be able to give her any answer.

By this time the young gentleman had changed her posture
from lying breadth to length-wise on the couch: but her thighs
were still spread, and the mark lay fair for him, who, now kneeling between them, display'd to us a side-view of that fierce erect
machine of his, which threaten'd no less than splitting the tender
victim, who lay smiling at the uplifted stroke, nor seem'd to
decline it. He looked upon his weapon himself with some pleasure, and guiding it with his hand to the invisible slit, drew aside
the lips, and lodg'd it (after some thrusts, which Polly seem'd
even to assist) about half way; but there it stuck, I suppose from
its growing thickness: he draws it again, and just wetting it with
spittle, re-enters, and with ease sheath'd it now up to the hilt, at
which Polly gave a deep sigh, which was quite another tone than
one of pain; he thrusts, she heaves, at first gently, and in a regular cadence; but presently the transport began to be too violent
to observe any order or measure; their motions were too rapid,
their kisses too fierce and fervent for nature to support such fury
long: both seem'd to me out of themselves: their eyes darted
fires: 'Oh! . . . oh! . . . I can't bear it . . . It is too much . . . I die
. . . I am going . . .' were Polly's expressions of ecstasy: his joys
were more silent; but soon broken murmurs, sighs heart-fetch'd,
and at length a dispatching thrust, as if he would have forced
himself up her body, and then motionless languor of all his limbs,
all shewed that the die-away moment was come upon him; which
she gave signs of joining with, by the wild throwing of her hands
about, closing her eyes, and giving a deep sob, in which she
seemed to expire in an agony of bliss.

When he had finish'd his stroke, and got from off her, she lay
still without the last motion, breathless, as it should seem, with
pleasure. He replaced her again breadth-wise on the couch,
unable to sit up, with her thighs open, between which I could
observe a kind of white liquid, like froth, hanging about the outward lips of that recently opened wound, which now glowed with
a deeper red. Presently she gets up, and throwing her arms round
him, seemed far from undelighted with the trial he had put her
to, to judge at least by the fondness with which she ey'd and
hung upon him.

For my part, I will not pretend to describe what I felt all over
me during this scene; but from that instant, adieu all fears of
what man could do unto me; they were now changed into such
ardent desires, such ungovernable longings, that I could have
pull'd the first of that sex that should present himself, by the
sleeve, and offered him the bauble, which I now imagined the loss
of would be a gain I could not too soon procure myself.

Phoebe, who had more experience, and to whom such sights

were not so new, could not however be unmoved at so warm a scene; and drawing me away softly from the peep-hole, for fear of being overheard, guided me as near the door as possible, all passive and obedient to her least signal.

Here was no room either to sit or lie, but making me stand with my back towards the door, she lifted up my petticoats, and with her busy fingers fell to visit and explore that part of me, where now the heat and irritations were so violent, that I was perfectly sick and ready to die with desire; the bare touch of her finger, in that critical place, had the effect of a fire to a train, and her hand instantly made her sensible to what a pitch I was wound up, and melted by the sight she had thus procured me.

BELOW The print entitled *The Curious Wanton* by Thomas Rowlandson (1756–1827). Although erotic subjects formed only a small part of his output, many are unforgettable images offering us his own uniquely ribald insights into the sexual manners of Regency England.

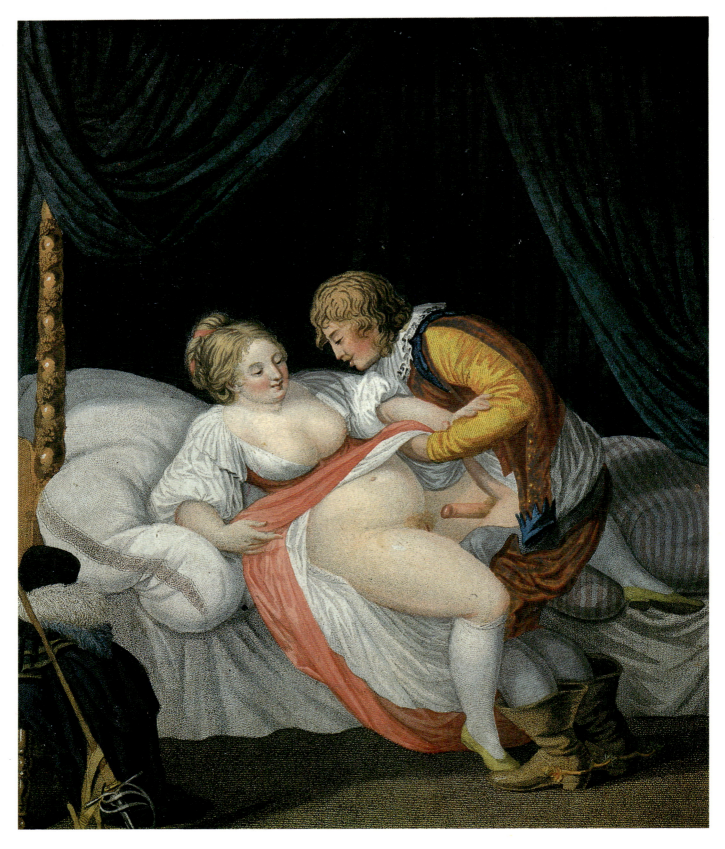

The tedious male preoccupation with 'being the first' (wonderfully lampooned in the song 'She Lost Her Virginity at the Astor Club': 'they found one on a pillow, but it wasn't hers') supported a minor industry at one time. The ingenuity of prostitutes whose maidenheads could be resurrected indefinitely to please their clownish clients has a certain gruesome humour, but we will not dwell too long on the subject of deflowering in this anthology. Octavia describes her initiation in one of the most famous erotic books of all time, Nicolas Chorier's *Satyra Sotadica*, which appeared in numerous versions in different languages from 1660 onwards. The vigour of the writing is typical of the seven dialogues between Octavia and her sexually experienced aunt Tullia.

Caviceo came on, blithe and joyous . . . He despoils me of my chemise, and his libertine hand touches my parts. He tells me to sit down again as I was seated before, and places a chair under either foot in such a way that my legs were lifted high in air, and the gate of my garden was wide open to the assaults I was expecting. He then slides his right hand under my buttocks and draws me a little closer to him. With his left he supported the weight of his spear. Then he laid himself down on me . . . put his battering-ram to my gate, inserted the head of his member into the outermost fissure, opening the lips of it with his fingers. But there he stopped, and for a while made no further attack. 'Octavia sweetest', he says, 'clasp me tightly, raise your right thigh and rest it on my side.' – 'I do not know what you want', I said. Hearing this he lifted my thigh with his own hand, and guided it round his loin, as he wished; finally he forced his arrow into the target of Venus. In the beginning he pushes in with gentle blows, then quicker, and at last with such force I could not doubt that I was in great danger. His member was hard as horn, and he forced it in so cruelly, that I cried out, 'You will tear me to pieces!' He stopped a moment from his work. 'I implore you to be quiet, my dear', he said, 'it can only be done this way; endure it without flinching'. Again his hand slid under my buttocks, drawing me nearer, for I had made a feint to draw back, and without more delay plied me with such fast and furious blows that I was near fainting away. With a violent effort he forced his spear right in, and the point fixed itself in the depths of the wound. I cry out . . . Caviceo spurted out his venerean exudation, and I felt irrigated by a burning rain . . . Just as Caviceo slackened, I experienced a sort of voluptuous itch as though I were making water; involuntarily I draw my buttocks back a little, and in an instant I felt with supreme pleasure something flowing from me which tickled me deliciously. My eyes failed me, my breath came thick, my face was on fire, and I felt my whole body melting. 'Ah! ah! ah! my Caviceo, I shall faint away', I cried; 'hold my soul – it is escaping from my body!'

OPPOSITE An eighteenth-century coloured etching.
BELOW Much of eighteenth-century French erotica was strongly anti-clerical in tone. Authors fired with the new materialism of the Enlightenment scattered their novels liberally with lecherous monks and debauched ecclesiastics.

Seduction, not unexpectedly, is a recurring theme in erotic literature. For the real-life erotomane ('Walter' or Casanova) who dedicates most of his time and energy to sex, it is variety which is important: not so much variety in lovemaking, which is of more interest and relevance to the monogamous, but an endless variety of 'conquests'. Unable to sustain more than a shallow and inevitably unsatisfactory relationship, they move rapidly from one partner to another. There is, of course, an underlying homosexuality about these serial lovers, both men and women. The saying that 'a man who cannot find what he wants in a thousand women is looking for a man' is very perceptive; it is interesting how many of Casanova's sexual exploits involve women who are dressed as men. Such careers tend not to have happy endings. The ageing Casanova, librarian to Count Waldstein in Dux, Bohemia, alone in the draughty room writing his famous *Memoirs,* is a rather pathetic figure. He never completed the work, but the *Memoirs* are a clever and apparently truthful account of his extraordinary life and times. Here Casanova recalls one of his more imaginative seductions, where a theological debate with two girls is quickly turned to his advantage. Hedwig, though quick intellectually, is not familiar with the word 'erection'.

'What is that?'

'Give me your hand.'

'I feel it, and it is as I had imagined it would be; for without this phenomenon of nature man could not impregnate his spouse. And that fool of a theologian maintains that it is an imperfection!'

'Yes, for the phenomenon arises from desire; witness the fact that it would not have taken place in me, beautiful Hedwig, if I had not found you charming, and if what I see of you did not give me the most seductive idea of the beauties I do not see. Tell me frankly if, on your side, feeling this stiffness does not cause you a pleasant excitation?'

'I admit it, and precisely in the place you are pressing. Do not you, my dear Helena, feel as I do a certain itching here while you listen to the very sound discourse to which Monsieur is treating us?'

'Yes, I feel it, but I feel it very often where there is no discourse to excite it.'

'And then,' I said, 'does not Nature oblige you to relieve it in this fashion?'

'Certainly not.'

'But it does!' said Hedwig. 'Even in sleep our hand goes there instinctively; and without that relief, I have read, we should be subject to terrible maladies.'

Continuing this philosophical discussion, which the young theologian sustained in a masterly manner and which gave her cousin's beautiful complexion all the animation of voluptuous feeling, we arrived at the edge of a superb basin of water with a flight of marble stairs down which one went to bathe. Though it

ABOVE Artists employed to illustrate the erotica of the Enlightenment often went far beyond their texts, employing a formidable armoury of technical and psychological effects to make the image as powerful as possible. The young woman here has not only been 'discovered', her solitary pleasure is also conveniently lit by her discoverer's candle.

was chilly our heads were heated, and it occurred to me to ask them to dip their feet in the water, assuring them that it would do them good and that, if they would permit me, I would have the honor of taking off their shoes and stockings.

'Why not?' said the niece. 'I'd like it.'

'So should I,' said Helena.

'Then sit down, ladies, on the top step.' And they sit, and I, placing myself on the fourth step below, fall to taking off their shoes and stockings, praising the beauty of their legs, and for the moment showing no interest in seeing anything above the knee. I took them down to the water, and then there was nothing for it but that they should pull up their dresses, and I encouraged them to do so.

'Well,' said Hedwig, 'men have thighs too.'

Helena, who would have been ashamed to show less courage than her cousin, was not slow to follow her example.

'Come, my charming Naiads,' I said, 'that is enough; you might catch cold if you stay in the water longer.'

They came up the stairs backward, still holding up their skirts for fear of wetting them; and it was my part to dry them with all the handkerchiefs I had. This agreeable office allowed me to see and to touch in perfect freedom, and the reader will not need to have me swear that I made the most of the opportunity. The beautiful niece told me that I was too curious, but Helena accepted my ministrations in a manner so tender and languishing that I

ABOVE Rowlandson, who had trained formally at the Royal Academy and in Paris, has fun with the familiar 'reclining Venus' pose. No wisp of material, draped hand, fruit or conch shell conceals the femininity of this Venus: as appealing to us as to her enthusiastic 'Apollo'.

had to use all my will to keep from going further. Finally, when I had put on their shoes and stockings, I said that I was in raptures at having seen the secret beauties of the two most beautiful girls in Geneva.

'What effect did it have on you?' Hedwig asked me.

'I do not dare tell you to look; but feel, both of you.'

'You must bathe too.'

'That is impossible, getting ready takes a man too long.'

'But we still have two full hours to stay here with no fear of anyone coming to join us.'

Her answer made me see all the good fortune which awaited me; but I did not choose to expose myself to an illness by entering the water in the state I was in. Seeing a garden house a short distance away and certain that Monsieur Tronchin would have left it unlocked, I took them there, not letting them guess my intention.

The garden house was full of pot-pourri jars, charming engravings, and so on; but what was best of all was a fine, large couch ready for repose and pleasure. Sitting on it between the two beauties and lavishing caresses on them, I told them I wanted to show them what they had never seen, and, so saying, I exposed to their gaze the principal effective cause of humanity. They stood up to admire me; whereupon, taking them each by one hand, I gave them a factitious consummation; but in the course of my labors an abundant emission of liquid threw them into the greatest astonishment.

'It is the word,' I said, 'the great creator of mankind.'

'How delicious!' cried Helena, laughing at the designation 'word'.

'But I too,' said Hedwig, 'have the word, and I will show it to you if you will wait a moment.'

'Sit on my lap, beautiful Hedwig, and I will save you the trouble of making it come yourself, and I will do it better than you can.'

'I believe you, but I have never done it with a man.'

'Nor have I,' said Helena.

Having made them stand in front of me with their arms around me, I made them faint again. Then we all sat down, and, while I explored their charms with my hands, I let them amuse themselves by touching me as they pleased, until I finally wet their hands with a second emission of the humid radical, which they curiously examined on their fingers.

After restoring ourselves to a state of decency, we spent another half hour exchanging kisses, then I told them they had made me half happy, but that to bring their work to completion I hoped they would think of a way to grant me their first favors. I then showed them the little protective bags which the English invented to free the fair sex from all fear. These little purses, whose use I explained to them, aroused their admiration, and the beautiful theologian told her cousin that she would think about it. Become intimate friends and well on the way to becoming something more, we made our way toward the house, where we found the pastor and Helena's mother strolling beside the lake.

ABOVE An etching by the German artist M. E. Phillipp.
OPPOSITE An unknown nineteenth-century artist (possibly Zichy or Charles de Beaumont) tries out some ideas for a study of fellatio. The vigour of the drawing and keenness of observation suggest that this – like Turner's erotic sketches tragically destroyed by Ruskin – may have been sketched from life.

Mixing theology with seduction can be dangerous, as the lecherous hermit Rustico learns to his cost in the delightful tale 'How the Devil is Put in Hell' from Boccaccio's *Decameron*, one of the earliest printed books. The deceiver takes advantage of a young girl's piety and naivety.

And so, setting forth again, she came at length to the cell of a young hermit, a worthy man and very devout, his name Rustico, whom she interrogated as she had the others. Rustico, being minded to make severe trial of his constancy, did not send her away, as the others had done, but kept her with him in his cell, and when night came, made her a little bed of palm-leaves; whereon he bade her compose herself to sleep. Hardly had she done so before the solicitations of the flesh joined battle with the powers of Rustico's spirit, and he, finding himself left in the lurch by the latter, endured not many assaults before he beat a retreat, and surrendered at discretion: whereupon he bade adieu to holy meditation and prayer and discipline, and fell a musing on the youth and beauty of his companion, and also how he might so order his conversation with her, that without seeming to her to be a libertine he might yet compass that which he craved of her. So, probing her by certain questions, he discovered that she was as yet entirely without cognizance of man, and as simple as she seemed: whereupon he excogitated a plan for bringing her to pleasure him under colour of serving God. He began by giving her a long lecture on the great enmity that subsists between God and the Devil; after which he gave her to

BELOW An untypically cheerful portrayal of the Devil by the Belgian etcher Félicien Rops. For the Decadents, among whom Rops was a powerful force, Satan symbolized the ultimate freedom from convention. Rops was a brilliant artist, his work much in demand. Ironically it was neither absinthe nor syphilis that killed him in 1898 but that most bourgeois of all angels of death – overwork.

understand that, God having condemned the Devil to hell, to put him there was of all services the most acceptable to God. The girl asking him how it might be done, Rustico answered: 'Thou shalt know it in a trice; thou hast but to do that which thou seest me do.' Then, having divested himself of his scanty clothing, he threw himself stark naked on his knees, as if he would pray; whereby he caused the girl, who followed his example, to confront him in the same posture. Whereupon Rustico, seeing her so fair, felt an accession of desire, and therewith came an insurgence of the flesh, which Alibech marking with surprise, said: – 'Rustico, what is this, which I see thee have, that so protrudes, and which I have not?' 'Oh! my daughter,' said Rustico, ''tis the Devil of whom I have told thee: and, seest thou? he is now tormenting me most grievously, insomuch that I am scarce able to hold out.' Then: – 'Praise be to God,' said the girl, 'I see that I am in better case than thou, for no such Devil have I.' 'Sooth sayst thou,' returned Rustico; 'but instead of him thou hast somewhat else that I have not.' 'Oh!' said Alibech, 'what may that be?' 'Hell,' answered Rustico: 'and I tell thee, that 'tis my belief that God has sent thee hither for the salvation of my soul; seeing that, if this Devil shall continue to plague me thus, then, so thou wilt have compassion on me and permit me to put him in hell, thou wilt both afford me exceeding great solace, and render to God an exceeding great and most acceptable service, if, as thou sayst, thou art come into these parts for such a purpose.' In good faith the girl made answer: – 'As I have hell to match your Devil, be it, my father, as and when you will.' Whereupon: – 'Bless thee, my daughter,' said Rustico, 'go we then, and put him there, that he leave me henceforth in peace.' Which said, he took the girl to one of the beds and taught her the posture in which she must lie in order to incarcerate this spirit accursed of God. The girl, having never before put any devil in hell, felt on this first occasion a twinge of pain: whereupon she said to Rustico: – 'Of a surety, my father, he must be a wicked fellow, this devil, and in very truth a foe to God; for there is sorrow even in hell – not to speak of other places – when he is put there.' 'Daughter,' said Rustico, ''twill not be always so.' And for better assurance thereof they put him there six times before they quitted the bed; whereby they so thoroughly abased his pride that he was fain to be quiet. However, the proud fit returning upon him from time to time, and the girl addressing herself always obediently to its reduction, it so befell that she began to find the game agreeable, and would say to Rustico: – 'Now see I plainly that 'twas true, what the worthy men said at Capsa, of the service of God being so delightful: indeed I cannot remember that in aught that ever I did I had so much pleasure, so much solace, as in putting the Devil in hell; for which cause I deem it insensate folly on the part of any one to have a care to aught else than the

service of God.' Wherefore many a time she would come to Rustico, and say to him: – 'My father, 'twas to serve God that I came hither, and not to pass my days in idleness: go we then, and put the Devil in hell.' And while they did so, she would now and again say: – 'I know not, Rustico, why the Devil should escape from hell; were he but as ready to stay there as hell is to receive and retain him, he would never come out of it.' So, the girl thus frequently inviting and exhorting Rustico to the service of God, there came at length a time when she had so thoroughly lightened his doublet that he shivered when another would have sweated; wherefore he began to instruct her that the Devil was not to be corrected and put in hell, save when his head was exalted with pride; adding, 'and we by God's grace have brought him to so sober a mind that he prays God he may be left in peace'; by

RIGHT With only himself to blame, Cupid's interruption of the proceedings in this wonderful photogravure print seems less than fair to the adventurous lovers.

which means he for a time kept the girl quiet. But when she saw that Rustico had no more occasion for her to put the Devil in hell, she said to him one day: – 'Rustico, if thy Devil is chastened and gives thee no more trouble, my hell, on the other hand, gives me no peace; wherefore, as I with my hell have holpen thee to abase the pride of thy Devil, so thou wouldst do well to lend me the aid of thy Devil to allay the fervent heat of my hell.' Rustico, whose diet was roots of herbs and water, was scarce able to respond to her demands: he told her that 'twould require not a few devils to allay the heat of hell; but that he would do what might be in his power; and so now and again he satisfied her; but so seldom that 'twas as if he had tossed a bean into the jaws of a lion. Whereat the girl, being fain of more of the service of God than she had, did somewhat repine.

To examine another aspect of sexual beginnings, we need to look at a literary form with a long pedigree including such notables as St Augustine and Jean-Jacques Rousseau. The confession – true or otherwise – is of course a natural vehicle for conveying erotic ideas because even those which are spurious often have an air of salacious intimacy about them. The anti-clerical erotica of the seventeenth and eighteenth centuries made much use of the confession and the confessional, straining the credulity of the reader somewhat, but this is mainly unpleasant stuff and will not be included. More interesting are the musings of the real life 'Walter' in the Prefaces to his extraordinary confession. The matter-of-fact tone gives a flavour of honesty.

ABOVE AND BELOW These drawings were the creation of a pneumatic age: Zeppelin founded his factory at Friedrichshafen in the same year of 1900. The world had to wait more than a decade for Freud's 'Passing of the Oedipus Complex' and nearer seventy years for Beryl Cook.

--------- PREFACE ---------

I began these memoirs when about twenty-five years old, having from youth kept a diary of some sort, which perhaps from habit made me think of recording my inner and secret life.

When I began it, had scarcely read a baudy book, none of which, excepting *Fanny Hill*, appeared to me to be truthful: that did, and it does so still; the others telling of recherché eroticisms or of inordinate copulative powers, of the strange twists, tricks, and fancies of matured voluptuousness and philosophical lewdness, seemed to my comparative ignorance as baudy imaginings or lying inventions, not worthy of belief; although I now know, by experience, that they may be true enough, however eccentric and improbable, they may appear to the uninitiated.

Fanny Hill's was a woman's experience. Written perhaps by a

woman, where was a man's written with equal truth? That book has no baudy word in it; but baudy acts need the baudy ejaculations; the erotic, full-flavored expressions, which even the chastest indulge in when lust, or love, is in its full tide of performance. So I determined to write my private life freely as to fact, and in the spirit of the lustful acts done by me, or witnessed; it is written therefore with absolute truth and without any regard whatever for what the world calls decency. Decency and voluptuousness in its fullest acceptance cannot exist together, one would kill the other; the poetry of copulation I have only experienced with a few women, which however neither prevented them nor me from calling a spade a spade . . .

I had from youth an excellent memory, but about sexual matters a wonderful one. Women were the pleasure of my life. I loved cunt, but also who had it; I like the woman I fucked and not simply the cunt I fucked, and therein is a great difference. I recollect even now in a degree which astonishes me, the face, colour, stature, thighs, backside, and cunt, of well nigh every woman I have had, who was not a mere casual, and even of some who were. The clothes they wore, the houses and rooms in which I had them, were before me mentally as I wrote, the way the bed and furniture were placed, the side of the room the windows were on, I remembered perfectly; and all the important events I can fix as to time, sufficiently nearly by reference to my diary, in which the contemporaneous circumstances of my life are recorded.

I recollect also largely what we said and did, and generally our baudy amusements. Where I fail to have done so, I have left description blank, rather than attempt to make a story coherent by inserting what was merely probable. I could not now account for my course of action, or why I did this, or said that, my conduct seems strange, foolish, absurd, very frequently, that of some women equally so, but I can but state what did occur . . .

. . . this is intended to be a true history, and not a lie.

Give me chastity and constancy, but not yet.

FROM *CONFESSIONS*
ST AUGUSTINE (354–430 AD)

ABOVE A study in erotic languor by M. E. Phillipp, a German artist much influenced by Beardsley and the Decadents. Though most did not themselves live to see it, the world of the Old Europe the Decadents so hated was about to end. This etching was completed just before the First World War.

─────── SECOND PREFACE ───────

Some years have passed away since I penned the foregoing, and it is not printed. . . . The manuscript has grown into unmanageable bulk; shall it, can it, be printed? What will be said or thought of me, what became of the manuscript if found when I am dead? Better to destroy the whole, it has fulfilled its purpose in amusing me, now let it go to the flames!

I have read my manuscript through; what reminiscences! I had actually forgotten some of the early ones; how true the detail strikes me as I read of my early experiences; had it not been written then it never could have been written now; has anybody but myself faithfully made such a record? It would be a sin to burn all this, whatever society may say, it is but a narrative of human life, perhaps the every day life of thousands, if the confession could be had . . .

Shall it be burnt or printed? How many years have passed in this indecision? why fear? it is for others' good and not my own if preserved.

Fanny Hill, although forbidden, was widely available at the time Walter confessed to reading it (in the 1850s). But how different in style and intention from his own obsessive catalogue. In this fragment Fanny Hill has extracted a confession from one of her colleagues, Louisa, regarding her beginnings.

BELOW Female auto-eroticism is a recurring theme in the art and literature of sexuality. The impulse is partly voyeuristic, but the confirmation of female sexual appetite also excites the male imagination.

'I now shunn'd all company in which there was no hopes of coming at the object of my longings, and used to shut myself up, to indulge in solitude some tender meditation on the pleasures I strongly perceiv'd the overture of, in feeling and examining what nature assur'd me must be the chosen avenue, the gates for unknown bliss to enter at, that I panted after.

'But these meditations only increas'd my disorder, and blew the fire that consumed me. I was yet worse when, yielding at length to the insupportable irritations of the little fairy charm that tormented me, I seiz'd it with my fingers, teasing it to no end. Sometimes, in the furious excitations of desire, I threw myself on the bed, spread my thighs apart, and lay as it were expecting the longed-for relief, till finding my illusion, I shut and squeez'd them together again, burning and fretting. In short, this devilish thing, with its impetuous girds and itching fires, led me such a life, that I could neither, night or day, be at peace with it or myself . . .

'But frequency of use dulling the sensation, I soon began to perceive that this work was but a paltry shallow expedient that went but a little way to relieve me, and rather rais'd more flame than its dry and insignificant titillation could rightly appease.

'Man alone, I almost instinctively knew, as well as by what I had industriously picked up at weddings and christenings, was possess'd of the only remedy that could reduce this rebellious disorder; but watch'd and overlook'd as I was, how to come at it was the point, and that, to all appearance, an invincible one; not that I did not rack my brains and invention how at once to elude my mother's vigilance, and procure myself the satisfaction of my impetuous curiosity and longings for this mighty and untasted pleasure. At length, however, a singular chance did at once the work of a long course of alertness. One day that we had dined at an acquaintance's over the way, together with a gentlewoman-lodger that occupied the first floor of the house, there started an indispensable necessity for my mother's going down to *Greenwich* to accompany her . . .

'As soon as she was gone, I told the maid I would go up and lie down on our lodger's bed, mine not being made, with a charge to her at the same time not to disturb me, as it was only rest I wanted. This injunction probably prov'd of eminent service to me. As soon as I was got into the bed-chamber, I unlaced my stays, and threw myself on the outside of the bedclothes, in all the loosest undress. Here I gave myself up to the old insipid privy shifts of my self-viewing, self-touching, self-enjoying, *in fine*, to all the means of *self-knowledge* I could devise, in search of the pleasure that fled before me, and tantalized with that unknown something that was out of my reach; this all only serv'd to enflame myself, and to provoke violently my desires, whilst the one thing needful to their satisfaction was not at hand, and I could have but my fingers, for representing it so ill. After then wearying and fatiguing myself with grasping shadows, whilst that most sensible part of me disdain'd to content itself with less than realities, the strong yearnings, the urgent struggles of nature towards the melting relief, and the extreme self-agitations I had used to come at it, had wearied and thrown me into a kind of unquiet sleep: for, if I tossed and threw about my limbs in proportion to the distraction of my dreams, as I had reason to believe I did, a bystander could not have help'd seeing all for love. And one there was it seems; for waking out of my very short slumber, I found my hand lock'd in that of a young man, who was kneeling at my bedside, and begging my pardon for his boldness: but that being a son to the lady to whom this bedchamber, he knew, belonged, he had slipp'd by the servant of the shop, as he supposed, unperceiv'd, when finding me asleep, his first ideas were to withdraw; but that he had been fix'd and detain'd there by a power he could better account for than resist.

'What shall I say? my emotions of fear and surprise were instantly subdued by those of the pleasure I bespoke in great

BELOW An eighteenth-century French miniature painted on ivory and entitled *Young Woman Asleep.*

presence of mind from the turn this adventure might take; he seem'd to me no other than a pitying angel, dropt out of the clouds: for he was young and perfectly handsome, which was more than even I had asked for; *man*, in general, being all that my utmost desires had pointed at. I thought then I could not put too much encouragement into my eyes and voice; I regretted no leading advances; no matter for his after opinion of my forwardness, so it might bring him to the point of answering my pressing demands of present case; it was not now with his thoughts, but his actions, that my business immediately lay. I rais'd then my head, and told him, in a soft tone, that tended to prescribe the same key to him, that his mamma was gone out and would not return till late at night: which I thought no bad hint; but as it prov'd, I had nothing of a novice to deal with. . . . Finding then that his kisses, imprinted on my hand, were taken as tamely as he could wish, he rose to my lips; and glewing his to them, made me so faint with overcoming joy and pleasure, that I fell back, and he with me, in course, on the bed, upon which I had, by insensibly shifting from the side to near the middle, invitingly made room for him. He is now lain down by me, and the minutes being too precious to consume in untimely ceremony, or dalliance, my youth proceeds immediately to those extremities, which all my looks, flushing, and palpitations, had assured him he might attempt without the fear of repulse: those rogues the men read us admirably on these occasions. I lay then at length panting for the imminent attack . . . whilst my thighs were, by an instinct of nature, unfolded to their best; and my desires had so thoroughly destroy'd all modesty in me that even their being now naked and all laid open to him was part of the prelude that pleasure deepn'd my blushes at, more than shame. But when his hand, and touches, naturally attracted to their centre, made me feel all their wantonness and warmth in and round it, oh! how immensely different a sense of things did I perceive there, than when under my own insipid handling! And now his waistcoat was unbuttoned, and the confinement of the breeches burst through, when out started to view the amazing, pleasing object of all my wishes, all my dreams, all my love, the king member indeed! I gaz'd at, I devoured it, at length and breadth, with my eyes intently directed to it, till his getting upon me, and placing it between my thighs, took from me the enjoyment of its sight, to give me a far more grateful one, in its touch, in that part where its touch is so exquisitely affecting. . . . And who could describe those feelings, those agitations, yet exalted by the charm of their novelty and surprise? when that part of me which had so long hunger'd for the dear morsel that now so delightfully crammed it forc'd all my vital sensations to fix their home there, during the stay of my beloved guest; who too soon paid me for his hearty welcome, in a dissolvent, richer far than that I have heard of some queen treating her paramour with, in liquify'd pearl, and ravishingly pour'd into me, where, now myself too much melted to give it a dry reception, I hail'd it with the warmest confluence on my side, amidst all those ecstatic raptures, not unfamiliar I presume to this good company!

ABOVE Pillboxes embellished with charming – and often humorous – erotic miniatures were popular in eighteenth-century Europe. These examples were made in Russia.

Confessions are akin to voyeurism. 'True' confessions may be considered to carry a stronger erotic charge because they are 'real' – but are they? All writing is an artifice. Erotic writing, which taps directly into the fantasies and unknown motives of both writer and reader, is to be regarded with the deepest suspicion by those intent on pursuing reality. In erotica of all kinds, 'truth' is no more than sauce added to an already spicy dish.

Frank Harris can be our guide. It is important to end this section on beginnings with a better understanding of the machinery of erotica before moving on to its other preoccupations and functions.

In the 1890s, having made a considerable fortune, Harris bought a villa in San Remo to finish his book on Shakespeare. With the help of a lecherous gardener he provided himself with what amounted to a harem of pretty local girls. This is the scene.

Not content with exploring their beautiful young bodies, Frank also wants to explore their minds, thus possessing them more completely. Questioning them about their current sexual feelings he feeds his own vanity and enjoys again his sexual encounters with them from a different perspective. Their earlier experiences are enjoyed vicariously of course and the entire confession underlines the fact that women do indeed have sexual appetites (a major preoccupation of eroticism). To cap it all, these are young girls not yet twenty – with all the ambivalent chords that strikes in the male breast. He understands a thing or two about the erotic, does Frank. And let us not forget that in writing this and choosing the extract from his book we are again enjoying what Frank did vicariously. So are you, at one remove again, in reading this! Little did Flora suspect just how many people stepped into that wardrobe with her.

The girls' confessions must now speak for themselves. These are about as near to (and far away from) the truth as you will get in erotic literature, but a very long way from Walter's diary/catalogue. Because it is Frank he romanticizes and idealizes the sex, and edits and adds bits as well: which are plain to see. There is nothing wrong in this. After all, the girls' confessions are as much about him as them.

FLORA

'They were sisters and very wild; I didn't like them at all. They were too rude and bold and very mean. Still they served a purpose. They used to strip and put me in bed and one of them rubbed vaseline or some sort of grease

between my legs, and the other looked on till her turn came. The sensation of being looked at was almost as good as the one of being rubbed . . . I certainly wasn't able to analyse the why and the wherefore of it all; I just knew I liked it. And then came the older girls; when I was about fifteen, a girl took me up to her room and locked the door; it was a sort of wardrobe room – small and pitch dark. I was old enough to realize then just what I was doing. She put my hand on her sex and I touched her as well as I could. I know I liked doing it. Naturally she was fully developed and somehow that was an added enjoyment for me. It did me harm in that I used to brood over it, gloat over it, enjoy my lewd thoughts – well, fifteen is too young for that, especially as I didn't need encouraging.'

'But why shouldn't you be encouraged?' I couldn't help asking.

'I was already too much inclined that way,' she replied.

'So much the better,' I went on; 'I can't understand the implied condemnation.'

'Nor can I,' she rejoined. 'It's merely habit, the customary way of thinking and speaking.

'You want to know everything: are girls' desires as vagrant as those of men? Yes, and quite as strong, I think; when, as a young girl, a man attracted me, a complete stranger – or showed me he wanted me, in the tram or anywhere, I used to cross my legs and press my thighs together and squeeze my sex till I came just as if I had used my hand; often I was all wet. There, you have the truth! . . .

'When the gardener left me in the bedroom that first morning, I noticed how fine the sheets were and the pretty pictures in the room: "When will he come?" I asked myself; "What will he do?" And my heart was in my mouth.

'Before you came in that first time to see me, the hope of you set all my pulses throbbing. I threw myself on the bed and thought about it, and thinking gradually brought about the feeling that demands satisfaction, so I satisfied it by touching myself – waiting for you: you dear, you!

'I've told you nothing about men, you say; but really, I had no experiences to speak of till I came here. My mother was always warning me of the consequences and the risk of having a child was always present.

'I often saw men in the town I could have liked, but we lived right out in the country, and till your gardener came and talked

ABOVE AND OPPOSITE Etchings by Mario Tauzin, an artist born in Paris in 1910.

to me and assured me there was no risk and a great deal of fun, I never gave myself to any man: you are first, and you know it, don't you, dear?

'One young fellow used to come out last summer from the town and we used to take long walks, and he said he loved me and was always touching my breasts and trying to excite me in fifty ways; but when I mentioned marriage, he sheered off. Men want pleasure and no ties and I don't blame them. If I were a man, I'd do the same: it's we women run the risk; but not with you, dear.

'Oh, now, often I can feel those slow long kisses of yours on my breasts and – I close my eyes and give myself to you: love is the best thing in the world . . .'

ADRIANA

Adriana's account was very like that of Flora's in the early years, but at first she was more outspoken.

'Passion – I'm made of it, a colt – wild, crazy, untamed colt – quick, rashly impulsive, savage – and yet I've emotion enough in me – high poetry; the violin, "flame in the skies of sunset" – all bring tears to my eyes: the rippling of a stream, the green foliage of trees, books and pictures – a deep, sweet world.

'Of course, it was an older girl who first taught me sensuality; I don't really think she ever touched me. It was quite a one-sided affair, but what I did to her gave me quite a little pleasure of my own. Of course, I didn't know what she did it for. I liked it and that was all that mattered to me.

'. . . From twelve to fourteen I was at school and developed a passion for one of the seniors. And while I would have been thrilled at a single touch of her fingers even on my hand, she never took even the very slightest notice of me. The sight of her thrilled me, and if she passed me and I felt her brush against me, it set my heart beating. But that sort of hero worship is very common at school.

'Another girl of my own age one night surprised me by asking me to accompany her into the bathroom. I went along wondering. She locked the door and then in a somewhat shamefaced fashion, asked me to touch her. I did, and she touched me. Both of us were highly excited, but we were interrupted, and somehow we never tried anything further afterwards.

'You ask me about exciting myself . . . I used to do it every Saturday night. Then I had an orgy, once a week; it was splendid. I used to think of some man who had attracted me or shown that he wanted me and I'd begin.

'One day in the tram a common man came in and threw himself down opposite me. Of a sudden I noticed that his trousers were unbuttoned and I saw his sex: it made me angry at first; he was so dirty and common. But as I stole glances at it, it excited me fearfully; I crossed my legs and squeezed my sex and at once I came. I could not help it: when I got out I was all streaming – wet to my knees.

'You ask me about my feelings. I have only to wait a very short time before I come, usually. But it all depends on the state of my

---

BELOW M. E. Phillipp's subtle etching drenches the background with dark detail, emphasizing the whiteness of the woman's flesh. The visual pivot is pubic hair – the more compulsive because the dark triangle is partly concealed.

I couldn't help it. I can resist everything except temptation.

FROM *LADY WINDERMERE'S FAN*
OSCAR WILDE (1854–1900)

mind. If there is not a good (I should say bad) atmosphere, it takes long, but if I feel really passionate – almost lewd – a minute will do it. And I can do it again perhaps three times, but that's the limit. My legs give way under me after that – so I judge I've had the best of myself; anyway I couldn't do more than that consecutively.

'No one thrill is ever exactly like the last; you soon learn to differentiate. Of course, they all recur, but never one after the other – and sometimes my favorite thrill comes most seldom; it is when all my muscles stiffen and grow rigid; it may not occur for days, even weeks.'

Naturally, I went to work at once to bring on the rigid paroxysm in Adriana and found no difficulty. 'You could not do it again,' she said, but in ten minutes I proved that I could bring about the rigid orgasm as often as I liked. In fact, once after bringing on the paroxysm three or four times, she burst out crying and laughing in a sort of wild hysteria that took me hours to quiet.

CLARA

'You want to know whether I have touched myself. Sure; all girls have. If they say they haven't, they lie; the silly fools. Why shouldn't we have pleasure when it's so easy?

'I remember my father took me once to the picture gallery in Genoa. I loved the pictures; but one had a young man in it who looked right at me. I got off next morning and went back to the gallery to my pictured lover. I could not help it; I sat down on the bench opposite to him and crossed my legs and squeezed my sex till I was wet. And when I went to bed that night I thought of him, and his lovely limbs and his great eyes, and I touched myself with my hand pretending it was him till I came again and again, and at last got so wild I just had to stop or I'd have screamed – but lots of girls are like that.

'I think I was one of the few who let a boy have me time and again. I could not resist: the truth is, I wanted him as much as he wanted me . . .'

I found Clara in many respects the most delightful of all the girls. She had really no reticences, and loved to show her sex and to talk about her intense sensations in the crudest terms; but she never invented or beautified anything, and this simplicity of truth in her was most attractive. When, for example, she said, 'When you have me I feel the thrills running all down my thighs to the knees,' she was plainly describing an immediate personal experience, and when she told me that merely hearing my voice in the villa made her sex open and shut, I could be sure it was the truth. And bit by bit this truth of reciprocated sensation grew on me, till I, too, was won by the novelty of the emotion. Clara was the most wonderful mistress of them all.

BELOW A Mario Tauzin etching from a series completed in 1930. The artist extracts the maximum suggestiveness from his line work, holding the composition together with the dark areas of hair which he has understood act as erotic magnets in art as in life.

PART TWO

The refinements of passion

RIGHT Stone lovers from the Lakshmana Temple in Khajuraho, India, built in the tenth century AD.

It was a night of sensual passion, in which she was a little startled and almost unwilling: yet pierced again with piercing thrills of sensuality, different, sharper, more terrible than the thrills of tenderness, but, at the moment, more desirable. Though a little frightened, she let him have his way, and the reckless, shameless sensuality shook her to her foundations, stripped her to the very last, and made a different woman of her. It was not really love. It was not voluptuousness. It was sensuality sharp and searing as fire, burning the soul to tinder.

Burning out the shames, the deepest, oldest shames, in the most secret places. It cost her an effort to let him have his way and his will of her. She had to be a passive, consenting thing, like a slave, a physical slave. Yet the passion licked round her, consuming, and when the sensual flame of it pressed through her bowels and breast, she really thought she was dying: yet a poignant, marvellous death.

She had often wondered what Abelard meant, when he said that in their year of love he and Héloïse had passed through all the stages and refinements of passion. The same thing, a thousand years ago: ten thousand years ago! The same on the Greek vases, everywhere! The refinements of passion, the extravagances of sensuality!

FROM *LADY CHATTERLEY'S LOVER*
D. H. LAWRENCE

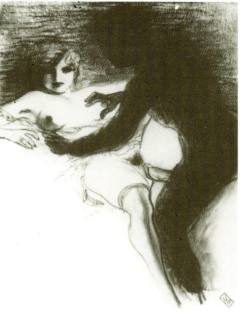

In this extract, while reflecting on the nature of erotic love during her post-coital 'high', Connie seizes upon the medieval lovers Abelard and Héloïse to express her sense of timelessness and of identification with all the lovers of the past. In fact there are other similarities between the experiences of the medieval lovers, expressed in their fascinating letters, and those of Lady Chatterley and her gamekeeper. It is just as well she kept her private thoughts from the unlettered Mellors, however, since he might have had a sleepless night. Peter Abelard (1079–1142) was a theologian who fell in love with his young pupil Héloïse. They had a child and married, which so infuriated her guardian that he had Abelard castrated. Following this disaster he became a monk, she a nun – the letters they later exchanged are among the jewels of European literature.

The conflict between sacred and 'profane' love is a Judaeo-Christian creation. In Hinduism, by way of contrast, sex is not regarded as tainted or disgraceful: in an everyday sense it is a pleasure to be enjoyed guiltlessly; theologically, the lovemaking of the God and Goddess, Shiva and Parvati, is the perfect expression of unity. In medieval India (and today in the subcontinent) male sexual organs – the lingam of Shiva – were worshipped; in medieval Europe, by contrast, they ran the risk of being cut off if they stepped out of line.

Christian theology recognizes that sacred and profane love come from the same spring – a nun is a 'bride of Christ' – but profane love must be transmuted, a process given expression in the figure of Mary Magdalene. This transmutation is not always perfect, however; there are ambiguities. In describing her religious ecstasy St Theresa wrote that an angel bearing a long burning spear with a fiery tip 'plunged it into my deepest innards. When he drew it out, I thought my entrails would have been drawn out too, and when he left me I glowed in the hot fire of love for God. The pain was so strong, and the sweetness thereof was so passing great, that no one could ever wish to lose it.' Bernini's famous sculpture of the saint in the Church of Santa Maria della Vittoria in Rome captures the moment she describes – and its ambiguity – perfectly. This is an old chestnut, and one occasionally pulled out of the fire by art historians. Is the expression Bernini gives her the ecstasy of sacred or profane love? 'Perhaps they look the same,' you may say. Perhaps they are the same.

ABOVE A drawing by the Austrian artist A1.
BELOW When Pope Clement VII (1478–1534) was late in paying an artist he unwittingly founded an erotic industry. The artist, Giulio Romano, retaliated by drawing a series of explicit sexual postures on the Vatican wall. These were then copied by Marcantonio and described by Aretino. Artists such as this sixteenth-century engraver were to produce their own versions of 'the postures' for the next 300 years.

ALCIBIADE ET GLYCERE.

Most Eastern religions avoid the painful riddle of sacred and profane love by regarding them as either the same, or aspects of the same phenomenon. Ikkyu was a Zen monk who achieved enlightenment at the age of twenty-six – there is a tradition that he was the illegitimate son of the Japanese emperor Gokomatsu. After the death of his spiritual mentor in 1428 Ikkyu began a life of wandering through a country experiencing the turmoil of civil war. For nearly half a century he devoted

his considerable energies to Zen Buddhism and wine, women and song – in about equal measure. Ikkyu's *Kyounshu*, a collection of poems written in Chinese, is among Japan's greatest works of literature. Much of his work was love poetry and many of these exquisite poems were written for Mori, the blind servant who became the greatest love of his life. It was a rather unconventional view, but for Ikkyu erotic passion and Zen were one and the same. Four different examples will illustrate what we mean.

Whispers, bashfulness and a pledge
We sing of love and make promises for three lives to come
We may fall to the way of beasts while still alive
But I shall surpass in passion the horned abbot of Kuei.

Blind Mori night after night sings with me
Under the covers, like mandarin ducks, new intimate talk
Making promises to be together till the dawning of Maitreya's
    salvation
At the home of this old buddha all is spring.

Rinzai's disciples don't understand Zen,
The truth was passed down to this blind donkey.
Making love for three lifetimes, ten aeons;
One night's autumn breeze a thousand centuries.

Dream-wandering in the garden of beautiful Mori,
A plum blossom in the bed, faith at the heart of the flower.
My mouth is filled with the pure fragrance of that shallow stream
Dusk and the shades of the moon as we make our new song.

OPPOSITE AND BELOW Japanese coloured woodcuts from the 1830s, known as Ukiyo-e or 'pictures of the floating world'.

Passionate love is one of the strongest emotions: it can move mountains and force kings into exile. The earth itself can move if Hemingway is to be believed (but who can feel quite the same about him after Gertrude Stein's savage put-down, 'false hair on the chest!'). If a Streetcar Named Desire hits you, what can be done? As always, the Hindu love manuals offer advice. Kalyana Malla wrote *Ananga-Ranga* a thousand years after *Kama Sutra*, although Vatsyayana's great work is still quoted.

But there are ten changes in the natural state of men, which require to be taken into consideration. Firstly, when he is in a state of Dhyasa at a loss to do anything except to see a particular woman; secondly, when he finds his mind wandering, as if he were about to lose his senses; thirdly, when he is ever losing himself in thought how to woo and win the woman in question; fourthly, when he passes restless nights without the refreshment of sleep; fifthly, when his looks become haggard and his body emaciated; sixthly, when he feels himself growing shameless and departing from all sense of decency and decorum; seventhly, when his riches take to themselves wings and fly; eighthly, when the state of mental intoxication verges upon madness; ninthly, when fainting fits come on; and tenthly, when he finds himself at the door of death.

That these states are produced by sexual passion may be illustrated by an instance borrowed from the history of bygone days. Once upon a time there was a king called Pururava, who was a devout man, and who entered upon such a course of mortification and austerities that Indra, Lord of the Lower Heaven, began to fear lest he himself might be dethroned. The god, therefore, in order to interrupt these penances and other religious acts, sent down from Svarga, his own heaven, Urvashi, the most lovely of the Apsaras (nymphs). The king no sooner saw her than he fell in love with her, thinking day and night of nothing but possessing her, till at last succeeding in his subject, both spent a long time in the pleasure of carnal connection. Presently Indra, happening

RIGHT An Indian miniature from Rajasthan.
OPPOSITE The favourite of a maharaja, painted in the late nineteenth century.

to remember the Apsara, dispatched his messenger, one of the Gandharvas (heavenly minstrels), to the world of mortals, and recalled her. Immediately after her departure, the mind of Pururava began to wander; he could no longer concentrate his thoughts upon worship and he felt upon the point of death.

See, then, the state to which that king was reduced by thinking so much about Urvashi! When a man has allowed himself to be carried away captive of desire, he must consult a physician, and the books of medicine which treat upon the subject. And, if he come to the conclusion that unless he enjoy his neighbour's wife he will surely die, he should, for the sake of preserving his life, possess her once and once only. If, however, there be no such peremptory cause, he is by no means justified in enjoying the

Dust of dead flowers, O tigress, has been spilled smoothly on the body of your breasts. It is a task to praise your breasts, for their tips are gilded like the sun and red like sunset.

FROM THE SANSCRIT
MAYURA, c. 800 AD

wife of another person, merely for the sake of pleasure and wanton gratification.

Moreover, the book of Vatsyayana, the Rishi, teaches us as follows: suppose that a woman, having reached the lusty vigour of her age, happen to become so inflamed with love for a man, and so heated by passion that she feels herself falling into the ten states before described, and likely to end in death attended with phrenzy, if her beloved refuse her sexual commerce. Under these circumstances, the man, after allowing himself to be importuned for a time, should reflect that his refusal will cost her life; he should, therefore, enjoy her on one occasion, but not always.

———————◊———————

Is passionate love a flower which is more likely to flourish in the gardens of others? There does seem to be a prevailing wind which often carries the seeds in that direction. In his wonderful poem, *Lone Gentleman*, the Chilean poet Pablo Neruda is uncompromising on the subject.

Young homosexuals and girls in love,
and widows gone to seed, sleepless, delirious,
and novice housewives pregnant some thirty hours,
the hoarse cats cruising across my garden's shadows
like a necklace of throbbing, sexual oysters
surround my solitary home
like enemies entrenched against my soul,
like conspirators in pyjamas
exchanging long, thick kisses on the sly.

The radiant summer entices lovers here
in melancholic regiments
made up of fat and flabby, gay and mournful couples:
under the graceful palm trees, along the moonlit beach,
there is a continual excitement of trousers and petticoats,
the crisp sound of stockings caressed,
women's breasts shining like eyes.

It's quite clear that the local clerk, bored to the hilt,
after his weekday tedium, cheap paperbacks in bed,
has managed to make his neighbour
and he takes her to the miserable flea-pits
where the heroes are young stallions or passionate
     princes:
he caresses her legs downy with soft hair
with his wet, hot hands smelling of cigarillos.

Seducer's afternoons and strictly legal nights
fold together like a pair of sheets, burying me:
the siesta hours when young male and female
     students
as well as priests retire to masturbate,
and when animals screw outright,
and bees smell of blood and furious flies buzz,
and cousins play kinkily with their girl cousins,
and doctors glare angrily at their young patient's husband,
and the professor, almost unconsciously, during the
     morning hours,
copes with his marital duties and then has breakfast,
and, later on, the adulterers who love each other with real love,
on beds as high and spacious as sea-going ships –
so for sure and for ever this great forest surrounds me,
breathing through flowers large as mouths chock full of teeth,
black-rooted in the shapes of hoofs and shoes.

ABOVE A charcoal drawing by the Viennese illustrator A1. OPPOSITE A twentieth-century oil painting on canvas by an unknown artist.

Sexual passion is not controllable – it rules us. It is no respecter of consequences, which is why it is so often tragic and the stuff of which great poetry is made. Thrones fall down like ninepins before it: we will pay any price, however high. In Tennyson's magnificent retelling of the Arthurian legend, *Idylls of the King*, we see how the whole machinery of Courtly Love, specifically designed to contain passion, is in fact destroyed by it. Sir Launcelot sacrifices honour and friendship, Queen Guinevere loses her husband and her freedom. Arthur's tragedy is not only the loss of his kingdom (and ultimately his life), but the fact that he still loves Guinevere. For us, of course, myths always embody truth. Saying his last farewell to Guinevere at the convent, the Queen's head bowed so that her long golden hair conceals her face, he whispers under his breath: 'Let no man dream but that I love thee still.'

Far away from Camelot, in their own Garden of Eden in Notting-

It's what the world would call very improper. But you know it's not really improper – I always labour at the same thing, to make the sex relation valid and precious, instead of shameful. And this novel is the furthest I've gone. To me it is beautiful and tender and frail as the naked self is.

ON *LADY CHATTERLEY'S LOVER*
D. H. LAWRENCE (1885–1930)

BELOW AND OPPOSITE Johannes Martini produced this series of remarkable charcoal drawings in Germany in 1915. He seems to have used models for the studies, but may have worked from photographs.

hamshire, Lady Chatterley and Mellors have their first encounter with passion, or he does. Afterwards she admits to herself that she 'had not been conscious of much' while for Mellors it was 'the old connecting passion'.

Connie crouched in front of the last coop. The three chicks had run in. But still their cheeky heads came poking sharply through the yellow feathers, then withdrawing, then only one beady little head eyeing forth from the vast mother-body.

'I'd love to touch them,' she said, putting her fingers gingerly through the bars of the coop. But the mother-hen pecked at her hand fiercely, and Connie drew back startled and frightened.

'How she pecks at me! She hates me!' she said in a wondering voice. 'But I wouldn't hurt them!'

The man standing above her laughed, and crouched down beside her, knees apart, and put his hand with quiet confidence slowly into the coop. The old hen pecked at him, but not so savagely. And slowly, softly, with sure gentle fingers, he felt among the old bird's feathers and drew out a faintly-peeping chick in his closed hand.

'There!' he said, holding out his hand to her. She took the little drab thing between her hands, and there it stood, on its impossible little stalks of legs, its atom of balancing life trembling through its almost weightless feet into Connie's hands. But it lifted its handsome, clean-shaped little head boldly, and looked sharply round, and gave a little 'peep'. 'So adorable! So cheeky!' she said softly.

The keeper, squatting beside her, was also watching with an amused face the bold little bird in her hands. Suddenly he saw a tear fall on to her wrist.

And he stood up, and stood away, moving to the other coop. For suddenly he was aware of the old flame shooting and leaping up in his loins, that he had hoped was quiescent for ever. He fought against it, turning his back to her. But it leapt, and leapt downwards, circling in his knees.

He turned again to look at her. She was kneeling and holding her two hands slowly forward, blindly, so that the chicken should run in to the mother-hen again. And there was something so mute and forlorn in her, compassion flamed in his bowels for her.

Without knowing, he came quickly towards her and crouched beside her again, taking the chick from her hands, because she was afraid of the hen, and putting it back in the coop. At the back of his loins the fire suddenly darted stronger.

He glanced apprehensively at her. Her face was averted, and she was crying blindly, in all the anguish of her generation's forlornness. His heart melted suddenly, like a drop of fire, and he put out his hand and laid his fingers on her knee.

'You shouldn't cry,' he said softly.

But then she put her hands over her face and felt that really her heart was broken and nothing mattered any more.

He laid his hand on her shoulder, and softly, gently, it began to travel down the curve of her back, blindly, with a blind stroking motion, to the curve of her crouching loins. And there his hand softly, softly, stroked the curve of her flank, in the blind instinctive caress.

She had found her scrap of handkerchief and was blindly trying to dry her face.

'Shall you come to the hut?' he said, in a quiet, neutral voice.

LEFT An oil painting by the German artist Paul Paede: born in Berlin in 1868, he died in Munich in 1929.

And closing his hand softly on her upper arm, he drew her up and led her slowly to the hut, not letting go of her till she was inside. Then he cleared aside the chair and table, and took a brown soldier's blanket from the tool chest, spreading it slowly. She glanced at his face, as she stood motionless.

His face was pale and without expression, like that of a man submitting to fate.

'You lie there,' he said softly, and he shut the door, so that it was dark, quite dark.

With a queer obedience, she lay down on the blanket. Then she felt the soft, groping, helplessly desirous hand touching her body, feeling for her face. The hand stroked her face softly, softly, with infinite soothing and assurance, and at last there was the soft touch of a kiss on her cheek.

She lay quite still, in a sort of sleep, in a sort of dream. Then she quivered as she felt his hand groping softly, yet with queer thwarted clumsiness, among her clothing. Yet the hand knew, too, how to unclothe her where it wanted. He drew down the thin silk sheath, slowly, carefully, right down and over her feet. Then with a quiver of exquisite pleasure he touched the warm soft body, and touched her navel for a moment in a kiss. And he had to come in to her at once, to enter the peace on earth of her soft,

Listen, the darkness rings
As it circulates round our fire,
Take off your things.

Your shoulders, your bruised throat!
Your breasts, your nakedness!
This fiery coat!

As the darkness flickers and dips,
As the firelight falls and leaps
From your feet to your lips!

FROM *NEW YEAR'S EVE*
D. H. LAWRENCE

OPPOSITE Portrait of a young
woman by an unknown artist, oil
on canvas, Austria, c. 1930.
BELOW Charcoal drawing by the
artist known as 'A1' (see page 13).

quiescent body. It was the moment of pure peace for him, the entry into the body of the woman.

She lay still, in a kind of sleep, always in a kind of sleep. The activity, the orgasm was his, all his; she could strive for herself no more. Even the tightness of his arms round her, even the intense movement of his body, and the springing of his seed in her, was a kind of sleep, from which she did not begin to rouse till he had finished and lay softly panting against her breast.

Then she wondered, just dimly wondered, why? Why was this necessary? Why had it lifted a great cloud from her and given her peace? Was it real? Was it real?

Her tormented modern-woman's brain still had no rest. Was it real? And she knew, if she gave herself to the man, it was real. But if she kept herself for herself, it was nothing. She was old; millions of years old, she felt. And at last, she could bear the burden of herself no more. She was to be had for the taking. To be had for the taking.

The man lay in a mysterious stillness. What was he feeling? What was he thinking? She did not know. He was a strange man to her, she did not know him. She must only wait, for she did not dare to break his mysterious stillness. He lay there with his arms round her, his body on hers, his wet body touching hers, so close. And completely unknown. Yet not unpeaceful. His very stillness was peaceful.

She knew that, when at last he roused and drew away from her. It was like an abandonment. He drew her dress in the darkness down over her knees and stood a few moments apparently adjusting his own clothing. Then he quietly opened the door and went out.

She saw a very brilliant little moon shining above the afterglow over the oaks. Quickly she got up and arranged herself; she was tidy. Then she went to the door of the hut.

All the lower wood was in shadow, almost darkness. Yet the sky overhead was crystal. But it shed hardly any light. He came through the lower shadow towards her, his face lifted like a pale blotch.

'Shall we go then?' he said.

'Where?'

'I'll go with you to the gate.'

He arranged things his own way. He locked the door of the hut and came after her.

'You aren't sorry, are you?' he asked, as he went at her side.

'No! No! Are you?' she said.

'For that! No!' he said. Then after a while he added: 'But there's the rest of things.'

'What rest of things?' she said.

'Sir Clifford. Other folks. All the complications.'

'Why complications?' she said, disappointed.

'It's always so. For you as well as for me. There's always complications.' He walked on steadily in the dark.

'And are you sorry?' she said.

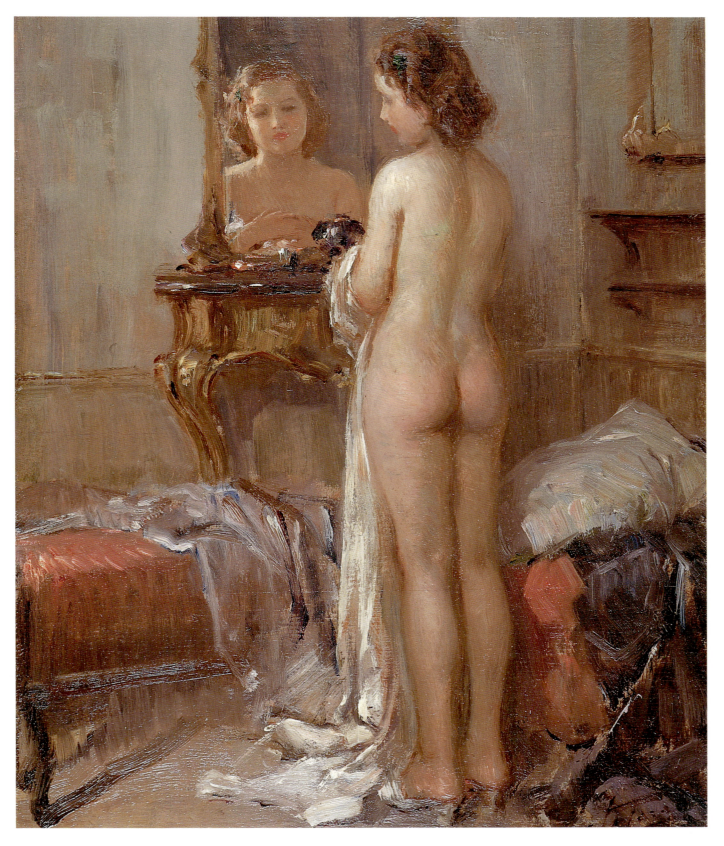

'In a way!' he replied, looking up at the sky. 'I thought I'd done with it all. Now I've begun again.'

'Begun what?'

'Life.'

'Life!' she re-echoed, with a queer thrill.

Recognition of her passion for Mellors, her husband's gamekeeper, comes later and suddenly to Lady Chatterley:

Ah, too lovely, too lovely! In the ebbing she realized all the loveliness. Now all her body clung with tender love to the unknown man, and blindly to the wilting penis, as it so tenderly, frailly, unknowingly withdrew, after the fierce thrust of its potency. As it drew out and left her body, the secret, sensitive thing, she gave an unconscious cry of pure loss, and she tried to put it back. It had been so perfect! And she loved it so!

And only now she became aware of the small, bud-like reticence and tenderness of the penis, and a little cry of wonder and poignancy escaped her again, her woman's heart crying out over the tender frailty of that which had been the power.

'It was so lovely!' she moaned. 'It was so lovely!' But he said nothing, only softly kissed her, lying still above her. And she moaned with a sort of bliss, as a sacrifice, and a newborn thing.

Fanny Hill has something to say on the subject of love and passion. On her first night in the house of her good-natured protector, though not at all averse to the delights of physical fulfilment, she is quite clear about the difference:

The maid, as soon as I was lain down, took the candle away, and wishing me a good night, went out of the room, and shut the door after her.

She had hardly time to get downstairs, before Mr. H . . . open'd my room door softly, and came in, now undress'd in his nightgown and cap, with two lighted wax candles, and, bolting the door, gave me, tho' I expected him, some sort of alarm. He came on tip-toe to the bedside, and said with a gentle whisper: 'Pray, my dear, do not be startled . . . I will be very tender and kind to you.' He then hurry'd off his clothes, and leap'd into bed, having given me openings enough, whilst he was stripping, to observe his brawny structure, strong-made limbs, and rough shaggy breast.

The bed shook again when it receiv'd this new load. He lay on the outside, where he kept the candles burning, no doubt for the satisfaction of ev'ry sense; for as soon as he had kiss'd me, he rolled down the bedclothes, and seemed transported with the view of all my person at full length, which he cover'd with a profusion of kisses, sparing no part of me. Then, being on his knees between my legs, he drew up his shirt, and bared all his hairy thighs, and stiff staring truncheon, red topp'd, and rooted into a thicket of curls, which covered his belly to the navel, and gave it

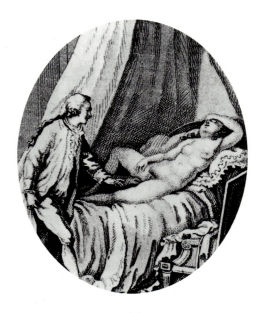

ABOVE AND BELOW Illustrations from an eighteenth-century French erotic novel. These were widely read throughout Europe, although in England translations were usually available soon after publication.

the air of a flesh brush; and soon I felt it joining close to mine, when he had drove the nail up to the head, and left no partition, but the intermediate hair on both sides.

I had it now, I felt it now, and, beginning to drive, he soon gave nature such a powerful summons down to her favourite quarters, that she could no longer refuse repairing thither; all my animal spirits then rush'd mechanically to that centre of attraction, and presently, inly warmed, and stirr'd as I was beyond bearing, I lost all restraint, and yielding to the force of the emotion, gave down, as mere woman, those effusions of pleasure, which, in the strictness of still faithful love, I could have wished to have help up.

Yet oh! what an immense difference did I feel between this impression of a pleasure merely animal, and struck out of the collision of the sexes, by a passive bodily effect, from that sweet fury, that rage of active delight which crowns the enjoyments of a mutual love-passion, where two hearts, tenderly and truly united, club to exalt the joy, and give it a spirit and soul that bids defiance to that end which mere momentary desires generally terminate in, when they die of a surfeit of satisfaction!

BELOW Doubting his stamina when confronted with a magnificent young derrière, an old rake seeks artificial aid. Rowlandson's print may be a satire of the contemporary vogue for taking the 'aphrodisiac' eryngoe.

Mr. H . . ., whom no distinctions of that sort seemed to disturb, scarce gave himself or me breathing time from the last encounter, but, as if he had task'd himself to prove that the appearances of his vigour were not signs hung out in vain, in a few minutes he was in a condition for renewing the onset; to which, preluding with a storm of kisses, he drove the same course as before, with unbated fervour; and thus, in repeated engagements, kept me constantly in exercise, till dawn of morning . . .

How different are Fanny's feelings when the stormy seas of Regency life return Charles, the love of her life, to her. There is a convention in erotic writing – even of the worst and ugliest kind – to rhapsodize about love. But Cleland is not doing that. If the prose seems ornate to a culture in which words are 'processed', the message was true and still is: 'the joy [of sex], great as it is, is still a vulgar one, whether in a king or a beggar; for it is, undoubtedly, love alone that refines, ennobles and exalts it.'

It is hard to imagine two more different writers than John Cleland and D. H. Lawrence, or two more different heroines than Fanny and Connie. But their feelings about the penis are strikingly similar. We have heard Lady Chatterley on the subject; this is Fanny Hill.

I have, I believe, somewhere before remark'd that the feel of that favourite piece of manhood has, in the very nature of it, something inimitably pathetic. Nothing can be dearer to the touch, nor can affect it with a more delicious sensation. Think then! as a love thinks, what must be the consummate transport of that quickest of our senses, in their central seat too! when, after so long a deprival, it felt itself re-inflam'd under the pressure of that peculiar sceptre-member, which commands us all: but especially, my darling, elect from the face of the whole earth. And now, at its mightiest point of stiffness, it felt to me something so subduing, so active, so solid and agreeable, that I know not what name to give its singular impression: but the sentiment of consciousness of its belonging to my supremely beloved youth gave me so pleasing an agitation, and work'd so strongly on my soul, that it sent all its sensitive spirits to that organ of bliss in me, dedicated to its reception. There, concentring to a point, like rays in a burning glass, they glow'd, they burnt with the intensest heat; the springs of pleasure were, in short, wound up to such a pitch, I panted now with so exquisitely keen an appetite for the eminent enjoyment, that I was even sick with desire, and unequal to support the combination of two distinct ideas, that delightfully distracted me: for all the thought I was capable of, was that I was now in touch at once with the instrument of pleasure and the great seal of love. Ideas that, mingling streams, pour'd such an ocean of intoxicating bliss on a weak vessel, all too narrow to contain it, that I lay overwhelm'd, absorb'd, lost in an abyss of joy, and dying of nothing but immoderate delight.

Charles then rous'd me somewhat out of this ecstatic distraction, with a complaint softly murmured, amidst a crowd of kisses, at the position, not so favourable to his desires, in which I receiv'd his urgent insistence for admission, where that insistence was alone so engrossing a pleasure, that it made me inconsistently suffer a much dearer one to be kept out; but how sweet to correct such a mistake! My thighs, now obedient to the intimations of love and nature, gladly disclose, and with a ready submission, resign up the soft gateway to the entrance of pleasure: I see, I feel the delicious velvet tip! . . . he enters me might and main, with . . . oh! my pen drops from me here in the ecstasy now present to my faithful memory! Description too deserts me, and delivers over a task, above its strength of wing, to the imagination: but it must be an imagination exalted by such a flame as mine that can do justice to that sweetest, noblest of all sensations, that hailed and accompany'd the stiff insinuation all the way up, till it was at the end of its penetration, sending up, through my eyes, the sparks of the love-fire that ran all over me and blaz'd in every vein and every pore of me; a system incarnate of joy all over.

I had now totally taken in love's true arrow from the point up to the feather, in that part, where making no new wound, the lips of the original one of nature, which had owed its first breathing to this dear instrument, clung, as if sensible of gratitude, in eager suction round it, whilst all its inwards embrac'd it tenderly, with a warmth of passion, a compressive energy, that gave it, in

ABOVE Engraving by an unknown artist, perhaps Antoine Borel (1743–1810).

its way, the heartiest welcome in nature; every fibre there gathering right round it, and straining ambitiously to come in for its share of the blissful touch.

As we were giving then a few moments of pause to the delectation of the senses, dwelling with the highest relish on this intimatest point of reunion, and chewing the cud of enjoyment, the impatience natural to the pleasure soon drove us into action. Then began the driving tumult on his side, and the responsive heaves on mine, which kept me up to him; whilst, as our joys grew too great for utterance, the organs of our voices, voluptuously intermixing, became organs of the touch . . . and oh, that touch! how delicious! . . . how poignantly luscious! . . . And now! now I felt, to the heart of me! I felt the prodigious keen edge, with which love, presiding over this act, points the pleasure: love! that may be styled the Attic salt of enjoyment; and indeed, without it, the joy, great as it is, is still a vulgar one, whether in a king or a beggar; for it is, undoubtedly, love alone that refines, ennobles and exalts it.

Thus happy, then, by the heart, happy by the senses, it was beyond all power, even of thought, to form the conception of a greater delight than what I was now consummating the fruition of.

Charles, whose whole frame was convulsed with the agitation of his rapture, whilst the tenderest fires trembled in his eyes, all assured me of a perfect concord of joy, penetrated me so profoundly, touch'd me so vitally, took me so much out of my own possession, whilst he seem'd himself so much in mine, that in a delicious enthusiasm, I imagin'd such a transfusion of heart and spirit, as that coalescing, and making one body and soul with him, I was he, and he, me.

BELOW Little English erotic literature was translated into French in the eighteenth century; the reverse was usually the case. *Fanny Hill* went against the tide and was even illustrated by the best of the French engravers.

The young Frank Harris wrestled with the problem of sex without love in his own muscular way. This is his first furious encounter with the voracious Mrs Mayhew, whose selfish passion, he confides later in *My Life and Loves*, 'chilled' him.

In a few minutes Miss Lily was playing a waltz on the Steinway and with my arm around the slight, flexible waist of my inamorata I was trying to waltz. But alas! after a turn or two I became giddy and in spite of all my resolutions had to admit that I should never be able to dance.

'You have got very pale,' Mrs. Mayhew said, 'you must sit down on the sofa a little while.' Slowly the giddiness left me; before I had entirely recovered Miss Lily with kindly words of sympathy had gone home, and Mrs. Mayhew brought me in a cup of excellent coffee; I drank it down and was well at once.

'You should go in and lie down,' said Mrs. Mayhew, still full of pity. 'See,' and she opened a door, 'there's the guest bedroom all ready.' I saw my chance and went over to her. 'If you'd come too,' I whispered, and then, 'The coffee has made me quite well: won't you, Lorna, give me a kiss? You don't know how often I said your name last night, you dear!' And in a moment I had again taken her face and put my lips on hers.

She gave me her lips this time and my kiss became a caress; but in a little while she drew away and said, 'Let's sit and talk; I want to know all you are doing.' So I seated myself beside her on the sofa and told her all my news. She thought I would be comfortable with the Gregorys. 'Mrs. Gregory is a good woman,' she added, 'and I hear the girl's engaged to a cousin: do you think her pretty?'

'I think no one pretty but you, Lorna,' I said, and I pressed her head down on the arm of the sofa and kissed her. Her lips grew hot: I was certain. At once I put my hand down on her sex; she struggled a little at first, which I took care should bring our bodies closer, and when she ceased struggling I put my hands up her dress and began caressing her sex: it was hot and wet, as I knew it would be, and opened readily.

But in another moment she took the lead. 'Some one might find us here,' she whispered. 'I've let the maid go: come up to my bedroom,' and she took me upstairs. I begged her to undress: I wanted to see her figure; but she only said, 'I have no corsets on; I don't often wear them in the house. Are you sure you love me, dear?'

'You know I do!' was my answer. The next moment I lifted her on to the bed, drew up her clothes, opened her legs and was in her. There was no difficulty and in a moment or two I came, but went right on poking passionately; in a few minutes her breath went and came quickly and her eyes fluttered and she met my thrusts with sighs and nippings of her sex. My second orgasm took some time and all the while Lorna became more and more

BELOW An anonymous French etching, c. 1920.

responsive, till suddenly she put her hands on my bottom and drew me to her forcibly while she moved her sex up and down awkwardly to meet my thrusts with a passion I had hardly imagined. Again and again I came and the longer the play lasted the wilder was her excitement and delight. She kissed me hotly, foraging and thrusting her tongue into my mouth. Finally she pulled up her chemise to get me further into her and, at length, with little sobs, she suddenly got hysterical and, panting wildly, burst into a storm of tears.

That stopped me: I withdrew my sex and took her in my arms and kissed her; at first she clung to me with choking sighs and streaming eyes, but, as soon as she had won a little control, I went to the toilette and brought her a sponge of cold water and bathed her face and gave her some water to drink – that quieted her. But she would not let me leave her even to arrange my clothes.

'Oh, you great, strong dear,' she cried, with her arms clasping me. 'Oh, who would have believed such intense pleasure possible: I never felt anything like it before; how could you keep on so long? Oh, how I love you, you wonder and delight.

'I am all yours,' she added gravely. 'You shall do what you like with me: I am your mistress, your slave, your plaything, and you are my god and my love! Oh, darling! Oh!'

At the time of the following sexual encounter with Kate, Mrs Mayhew had thrown in the sponge, which is as well since Harris needs it to revive his new mistress after the rigours of his lovemaking.

We got to the hotel about ten and bold as brass I registered as Mr. and Mrs. William Wallace and went up to our room with Kate's luggage, my heart beating in my throat. Kate, too, was 'all of a quiver,' as she confessed to me a little later, but what a night we had! Kate resolved to show me all her love and gave herself to me passionately, but she never took the initiative, I noticed, as Mrs. Mayhew used to do.

At first I kissed her and talked a little, but as soon as she had arranged her things, I began to undress her. When her chemise fell, all glowing with my caressings, she asked, 'You really like that?' and she put her hand over her sex, standing there naked like a Greek Venus. 'Naturally,' I exclaimed, 'and these, too,' and I kissed and sucked her nipples until they grew rosy-red.

'Is it possible to do it – standing up?' she asked, in some confusion.

'Of course,' I replied. 'Let's try! But what put that into your head?'

'I saw a man and a girl once behind the church near our house,' she whispered, 'and I wondered how –' and she blushed rosily. As I got into her, I felt difficulty: her pussy was really small and this time seemed hot and dry: I felt her wince and, at once, withdrew. 'Does it still hurt, Kate?' I asked.

'A little at first,' she replied. 'But I don't mind,' she hastened to add, 'I like the pain!'

They are not long, the days of wine and
*   roses . . .*
They are not long, the weeping and the
*   laughter,*
Love and desire and hate.
I think they have no portion in us after
We pass the gate.

FROM *DAYS OF WINE AND ROSES/VITAE SUMMA BREVIS*
ERNEST DOWSON (1867–1900)

By way of answer, I slipped my arms around her, under her bottom, and carried her to the bed. 'I will not hurt you tonight,' I said, 'I'll make you give down your love-juice first and then there'll be no pain.'

A few kisses and she sighed: 'I'm wet now,' and I got into bed and put my sex against hers.

'I'm going to leave everything to you,' I said, 'but please don't hurt yourself.' She put her hand down to my sex and guided it in, sighing a little with satisfaction as bit by bit it slipped home.

After the first ecstasy, I got her to use the syringe while I

RIGHT An anonymous French etching.

Darling, each morning a blooded rose
Lures the sunlight in, and shows
Her soft, moist and secret part.
See now, before you go to bed,
Her skirts replaced, her deeper red –
A colour much like yours, dear heart.

Alas, her petals will blow away,
Her beauties in a single day
Vanish like ashes on the wind.
O savage Time! that what we prize
Should flutter down before our eyes –
Who also, late or soon, descend.

FROM CORINNA IN VENDÔME
PIERRE DE RONSARD (1524–85)

watched her curiously. When she came back to bed, 'No danger now,' I cried, 'no danger; my love is queen!'

'You darling lover!' she cried, her eyes wide, as if in wonder. 'My sex throbs and itches and oh! I feel prickings on the inside of my thighs: I want you dreadfully, Frank,' and she stretched out as she spoke, drawing up her knees.

I got on top of her and softly, slowly let my sex slide into her and then began the love-play. When my second orgasm came, I indulged myself with quick, short strokes, though I knew that she preferred the long slow movement, for I was resolved to give her every sensation this golden night. When she felt me begin again the long slow movement she loved, she sighed two or three times and putting her hands on my buttocks, drew me close but otherwise made little sign of feeling for perhaps half an hour. I kept right on; the slow movement now gave me but little pleasure: it was rather a task than a joy; but I was resolved to give her a feast. I don't know how long the bout lasted, but once I withdrew and began rubbing her clitoris and the front of her sex, and panting she nodded her head and rubbed herself ecstatically against my sex, and after I had begun the slow movement again, 'Please, Frank!' she gasped, 'I can't stand more: I'm going crazy – choking!'

Strange to say, her words excited me more than the act: I felt my spasm coming and roughly, savagely I thrust in my sex at the same time, kneeling between her legs so as to be able to play back and forth on her tickler as well. 'I'll ravish you!' I cried and gave myself to the keen delight. As my seed spirted, she didn't speak, but lay there still and white; I jumped out of the bed, got a spongeful of cold water and used it on her forehead.

At once, to my joy, she opened her eyes. 'I'm sorry,' she gasped, and took a drink of water, 'but I was so tired, I must have slept. You dear heart!' When I had put down the sponge and glass, I slipped into her again and in a little while she became hysterical: 'I can't help crying, Frank, love,' she sighed. 'I'm so happy, dear. You'll always love me? Won't you? Sweet!' Naturally, I reassured her with promises of enduring affection and many kisses. Finally, I put my left arm round her neck and so fell asleep with my head on her soft breast.

ABOVE An etching Leon Richet made in 1880 to illustrate the Decadent writer Jules Barbey d'Aurévilly's collection of short stories *Les Diaboliques*.

One-sided passion, or detachment on the part of one of the protagonists, makes for unsatisfactory erotic writing. But then Frank Harris was writing about actual events. This exuberant piece from *The Boudoir*, which makes no claim for authenticity and is pure Victorian melodrama, was written specifically to excite the reader's erotic imagination: a kind of writing which is itself a sexual act.

We were in a small reception room that served as my boudoir. F., who understood me, went out and waited for me in the big drawing room, whither I rejoined him, with an odd volume in my hand.

ABOVE An illustration from *Les Diaboliques* (The Possessed), a savage satire on the foibles and sexual habits of Second Empire society.
RIGHT One of a series of charming watercolours by the Belgian artist Louis Morin.

In an instant, he declared his passion. What he said – what I answered, I know not. I remember nothing.

I led him towards the hall, for fear we should be overheard. There was a double door between the drawing room and a little vestibule, where I could hear a servant. As we reached there, Monsieur F., beside himself, seized me in his arms, and a lingering kiss, a kiss of fire, a kiss that responded to my soul, arrested a shriek that I should not have been able to stifle.

At the same time, his prompt hand had lifted my petticoats, and was scientifically caressing my burning slit, that quick as lightning poured out upon his fingers palpable traces of the spendings that filled it to overflowing.

'Begone, . . . begone! . . . away,' I said, with stifled accents. 'Go . . . To-morrow . . . three o'clock'; and I fled in a state which I cannot describe.

Happily, the lady who was waiting was not very clever, and did not notice my disordered state.

I shall not undertake to narrate my feelings till the next day. All that I can remember is, that I firmly resolved to satisfy my erotic longings.

My husband intended to absent himself for two or three days, and I arranged so as to send my servants on different errands. I dressed myself carefully and waited.

My dear F. arrived. I opened the door to him myself, and led him to my boudoir.

We sat down, much embarrassed. He was very respectful and asked my pardon for what he had done the day before, saying that he was unable to master the delirious rage that had seized him, and that his love for me was such that he would die if he was unable to enjoy me.

I knew not how to answer. Both our hearts were too full. He took my hand and kissed it. Shuddering, I rose. Our mouths met. I confess I made no more attempts at resistance. I had not the strength to do so.

I fully enjoyed this intense happiness. I felt that he was carrying me along – but to where? What were we to do? In my boudoir there were only a very narrow low sofa, some armchairs, and ordinary seats without arms.

F., still holding me in his arms, sat on a chair, so that I found myself in front of him, leaning over his head and face. I felt one of his arms loose my waist; soon my clothes were all up in front, and F. tried to pass his knees between my legs.

'Oh, no,' said I, between two sobs. 'No, . . . I pray you, have pity.'

F. made efforts to pull me down, so as to straddle across him; but on instinctive feeling, although I longed for it, I still resisted, and stiffened myself against him. We soon became exhausted. At last, having dropped my eyes a little, I saw something that put an end to the struggle.

F. had taken out his instrument for the fray. Its ruby, haughty head stood up proudly. In length and thickness really uncommon, it vied even with that of Monsieur B. I had no strength to resist such a sight; my thighs opened by themselves. I slid down hiding

my face on my lover's shoulder, and I gave myself up to him, opening myself as much as possible, desiring, and yet fearing the entrance of such a handsome guest.

I soon felt the head between the lips of my grotto, that the thin tool of my husband had not accustomed to such a bountiful measure. I made a movement to help him, and had hardly introduced the point, when I felt myself flooded by a flaming jet of loving liquor that covered thighs and belly.

The prolonged wait, and his own passion, had made the precious dew pump up too quickly, and I had not been able to enjoy it as I should.

I could not help showing a little disappointment, but my lover, covering me with kisses, told me that I need wait but during a brief period of repose, and that I should soon be more satisfied with him.

We sat on the sofa, entwined in each other's arms, telling one another of our love and happiness; we had fallen in love at first sight, and both had given way to irresistible passion.

In a few moments I saw that my lover was ready to begin again, and I asked how we were going to do it. I did not wish to try again that posture that had turned out so badly for me, and I could see F. also looking about him.

An idea struck me. I rose, smiling, and toying with him; he rose too, I retreated, and he eagerly pursued me, till at last I went and leant with nonchalance upon the mantelpiece, presenting my crupper, that I wriggled like a cat, and at the same time I turned my head and threw him a provoking glance.

Ah! how he understood me. F. rushed upon me, and kissed me, saying 'thank you.'

Then he got behind me, and threw my petticoats over my back. When he saw the beautiful shape of my bottom, he gave a loud cry of admiration. I expected as much, but did not dream of the homage he paid to it.

F. threw himself onto his knees, and after having covered my backside with kisses he drew them apart, just at the top of the thighs, and I could feel his lips, nay even his tongue. I shrieked out, and was overcome.

F. rose up, and began to put it in; his enormous instrument could not easily penetrate, in spite of our mutual efforts, so he drew it out, put a little saliva on the head and shaft, and I soon felt myself stabbed to the very vitals, filled and plugged tightly up, and in a state of unspeakable ecstasy.

My lover, leaning over me, glued his lips to mine, that I offered to him by turning my head; his tongue dallied with mine. I was beside myself. I felt myself going mad. The supreme moment arrived. I writhed about, uttering inarticulate words.

BELOW AND OPPOSITE In the preface to *Les Diaboliques*, published in 1873, the novel from which these illustrations are taken, the author explains the Decadent credo with heavy irony: '. . . real stories of this era of progress, of this civilization of ours which is so delicious and so divine that when one tries to write about it the Devil always seems to be dictating!'

A woman on her knees – Love only
*   knows*
What service she attends – to heaven
*   shows*
The artless epic of her shining seat.
Beauty's clear mirror, where she loves
*   to gaze,*
See and believe herself. O woman's
*   arse,*
Roundly defeating man's in every
*   class,*
O arse of arses: Glory! Worship!
*   Praise!*

FROM *A Brief Moral*
Paul Verlaine (1844–96)

F., who was reserving himself, was delighted at my joy; he let me calm down, and then I felt his sweet movement again.

Ah, how he knew how to distil pleasure, and double it by a thousand delicate, subtle shades. Oh! that first lesson; I can feel it, as I write, between my thighs.

'Dear angel,' he said, 'tell me what you feel; it's so nice to enjoy each other's soft confidence, when we form but one body, as at this moment.'

Oh, how his speech made me happy; I, who had always wished to hear and say those words that had almost driven me wild, when my aunt was at work! I did not hesitate an instant longer.

I have been a slave to my passions,
but never to a man!

LA BELLE OTÉRO
THE FAMOUS COURTESAN OF THE *BELLE EPOQUE*

'I must do it again,' said I, 'it's coming – push in – again – right in – finish me – ah! I die!'

'My adored one, I'm coming too – it's bubbling up – Ah I spend!'

F. gave a push, and fell upon me. I felt his ejaculation, and nearly fainted under the jet.

How was it that I did not die during that embrace? Nothing that I had imagined at the sight of my aunt's sweet struggles could approach this reality! I remained overwhelmed, my head in my arms, my bosom heaving, incapable of movement.

F. drew out. I still spent. I kept on spending. I stopped as I was, without sense of shame, naked to the waist, trembling, mechanically continuing the movement of my bottom, and causing the overflow of liquid to fall to the ground.

F. took pity on me. After rapidly adjusting himself, he pulled down my petticoats, and taking me in his arms sat by my side on the sofa. I was delirious for a second. He calmed me; his sweet voice brought me to a little. I begged him to leave me to myself, and he went away.

———————◇———————

The French watercolour (OPPOSITE) and etching (BELOW) are both by anonymous artists working in Paris during the 1920s.

Detachment, which as we have seen normally signals failure in the writing of erotica, is a key element in the highly individualistic style of Anaïs Nin. She somehow uses an artificial distancing to heighten the erotic effect, turning her best short stories into something approaching erotic fables or fairy stories. The man for whom she wrote repeatedly told her to 'leave out the poetry', evoking this furious response – a letter he would never have received, but which says some important things about the male and female perceptions of erotica:

Dear Collector: We hate you. Sex loses all its power and magic when it becomes explicit, mechanical, overdone, when it becomes a mechanistic obsession. It becomes a bore. You have taught us more than anyone I know how wrong it is not to mix it with emotion, hunger, desire, lust, whims, caprices, personal ties, deeper relationships that change its color, flavor, rhythms, intensities.

You do not know what you are missing by your microscopic examination of sexual activity to the exclusion of aspects which are the fuel that ignites it. Intellectual, imaginative, romantic, emotional. This is what gives sex its surprising textures, its subtle transformations, its aphrodisiac elements. You are shrinking your world of sensations. You are withering it, starving it, draining its blood.

If you nourished your sexual life with all the excitements and adventures which love injects into sensuality, you would be the most potent man in the world. The source of sexual power is curiosity, passion. You are watching its little flame die of asphyxiation. Sex does not thrive on monotony. Without feeling, inventions, moods, no surprises in bed. Sex must be mixed with tears, laughter, words, promises, scenes, jealousy, envy, all the spices of fear, foreign travel, new faces, novels, stories, dreams, fantasies, music, dancing, opium, wine.

How much do you lose by this periscope at the tip of your sex, when you could enjoy a harem of distinct and never-repeated wonders? No two hairs alike, but you will not let us waste words on a description of hair; no two odors, but if we expand on this you cry Cut the poetry. No two skins with the same texture, and never the same light, temperature, shadows, never the same gesture; for a lover, when he is aroused by true love, can run the gamut of centuries of love lore. What a range, what changes of age, what variations of maturity and innocence, perversity and art . . .

We have sat around for hours and wondered how you look. If you have closed your senses upon silk, light, color, odor, character, temperament, you must be by now completely shriveled up. There are so many minor senses, all running like tributaries into the mainstream of sex, nourishing it. Only the united beat of sex and heart together can create ecstasy.

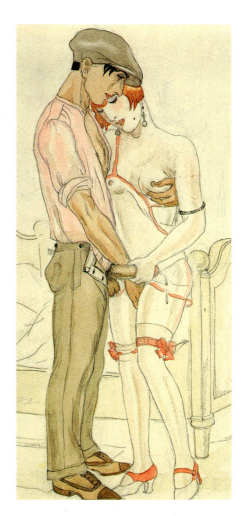

The erotica of Anaïs Nin, although among the best work in the genre and unusual for having been written by a woman, does not always live up to her aspirations for it. Some of this must be laid at the door of her literary tormentor ('leave out the poetry!'); but compare this extract from her short story *Elena* with the piece from *Lady Chatterley's Lover* which follows it and is similarly isolated from its context.

These were the external feelings of the bodies discovering each other. From so much touching they grew drugged. Their gestures were slow and dreamlike. Their hands were heavy. His mouth never closed.

How the honey flowed from her. He dipped his fingers in it lingeringly, then his sex, then he moved her so that she lay on him, her legs thrown over his legs, and as he took her, he could see himself entering into her, and she could see him too. They saw their bodies undulate together, seeking their climax. He was waiting for her, watching her movements.

Because she did not quicken her movements, he changed her position, making her lie back. He crouched over so that he could take her with more force, touching the very bottom of her womb, touching the very flesh walls again and again, and then she experienced the sensation that within her womb some new cells awakened, new fingers, new mouths, that they responded to his entrance and joined in the rhythmic motion, that this suction was becoming gradually more and more pleasurable, as if the friction had aroused new layers of enjoyment. She moved quicker to bring the climax, and when he saw this, he hastened his motions inside of her and incited her to come with him, with words, with his hands caressing her, and finally with his mouth soldered to hers, so that the tongues moved in the same rhythm as the womb and penis, and the climax was spreading between her mouth and her sex, in cross-currents of increasing pleasure, until she cried out, half sob and half laughter, from the overflow of joy through her body.

———— ◊ ————

He too had bared the front part of his body and she felt his naked flesh against her as he came into her. For a moment he was still inside her, turgid there and quivering. Then as he began to move, in the sudden helpless orgasm, there awoke in her new strange thrills rippling inside her. Rippling, rippling, rippling, like a flap-

BELOW A drawing by an unknown English artist.

ping overlapping of soft flames, soft as feathers, running to points of brilliance, exquisite, exquisite and melting her all molten inside. It was like bells rippling up and up to a culmination. She lay unconscious of the wild little cries she uttered at the last. But it was over too soon, too soon, and she could no longer force her own conclusion with her own activity. This was different, different. She could do nothing. She could no longer harden and grip for her own satisfaction upon him. She could only wait, wait and moan in spirit as she felt him withdrawing, withdrawing and contracting, coming to the terrible moment when he would slip out of her and be gone. Whilst all her womb was open and soft, and softly clamouring, like a sea-anemone under the tide, clamouring for him to come in again and make a fulfilment for her. She clung to him unconscious in passion, and he never quite slipped from her, and she felt the soft bud of him within her stirring, and strange rhythms flushing up into her with a strange rhythmic growing motion, swelling and swelling till it filled all her cleaving consciousness, and then began again the unspeakable motion that was not really motion, but pure deepening whirlpools of sensation swirling deeper and deeper through all her tissue and consciousness, till she was one perfect concentric fluid of feeling, and she lay there crying in unconscious inarticulate cries. The voice out of the uttermost night, the life! The man heard it beneath him with a kind of awe, as his life sprang out into her. And as it subsided, he subsided too and lay utterly still, unknowing, while her grip on him slowly relaxed, and she lay inert. And they lay and knew nothing, not even of each other, both lost.

◊

Language's taboo words are the stock in trade of the second-rate writer of erotica. The best-known Victorian underground magazine, *The Pearl*, was characterized by the excessive use of four-letter words which were used like strong spices to pepper up what is often a stale or indifferent dish. The short-lived *Boudoir* is more controlled in its use of strong language and is all the better for it. In this cleverly-crafted piece of hack work it is the overlooked lovers themselves who use language for their own amusement, so that both the visual and the auditory voyeurism is doubled up for the reader.

I shall not speak of the events of the day, which was an uninteresting one, as I am in haste to come to the scene of the evening. I took the same precautions, and had safely reached my observatory when Bertha and her lover met once more.

The preliminaries were much about the same, but instead of going to bed afterwards, Bertha said: 'I have a whim, dear. Let us do it like the other morning in the closet. We are more comfortable here, and it will be nicer still!'

With these words she divested herself of her gown, pulled up her shift behind, and placing a big cushion in front of the mirror of the wardrobe, she knelt upon it, her head and arms much lower than her

Where there is real sex there is the underlying passion for fidelity . . .

D. H. LAWRENCE (1885–1930)

◊

ABOVE A watercolour by the Viennese court painter Peter Fendi (1796–1842).

◊

buttocks, which, thrown out and developed by this ravishing position, presented the path of pleasure well in view and largely open.

Alfred, far from idle, had made his preparations. He had taken off his jacket and placed the lamp on the floor, so as to light up perfectly the delicious picture that the looking glass reflected in every detail. Then he placed himself behind her, and began to get into her.

'Oh, you can see too much of me!' said my aunt.

'How can I see too much of such beauties? Look in the glass!'

'Oh, no; it's too bad! . . . Ah! . . . It's going into me! Stop a little . . . What a fine fellow you are!'

'My adored one, how lovely you are! What admirable hips! What an adorable – ARSE!'

'Oh! Alfred! What is that naughty word?'

'Don't be frightened, darling; lovers can say anything. Those words, out of place in colder moments, add fresh relish to the sweet mystery of love? You will soon say them too, and understand their charm.'

While he spoke he continued his movements. Bertha, in silent enjoyment, said naught, but devoured with eager eyes the scene in the glass. I was stupefied to hear her say to him a minute later:

'Do you love it so very much?'

'What?'

'Why . . . my . . .'

'Your what?'

'Well . . . my . . . ARSE!'

'Ah, Bertha, how sweet you are to me. Oh, yes; I love it. Your beautiful arse. I adore it!'

'Feel it then. It's yours – yours alone. My arse – arse – arse. Oh, . . . my . . . arse, my arse!'

As she concluded her broken utterances, she let herself go till she reached complete enjoyment. Alfred, who was rapidly arriving at the height of sovereign pleasure, reached the desired goal with her, and fell upon her completely overcome.

———————◊———————

In the hands of a great writer taboo words can be used to their full effect, as in this extract from Molly Bloom's famous soliloquy at the end of James Joyce's *Ulysses*. Stripped of punctuation, and full of endless internal resonances, it pushes language to its limit.

. . . theres the mark of his teeth still where he tried to bite the nipple I had to scream out arent they fearful trying to hurt you I had a great breast of milk with Milly enough for two what was the reason of that he said I could have got a pound a week as a wet nurse all swelled out the morning that delicate looking student that stopped in No 28 with the Citrons Penrose nearly caught me washing through the window only for I snapped up the towel to my face that was his studenting hurt me they used to weaning her till he got doctor Brady to give me the Belladonna prescrip-

———————◊———————

Unless we know that they were working to a specific brief, it is reasonable to suppose that artists reveal a good deal about their own sexual proclivities in their erotic output. Perhaps it is no accident that Peter Fendi (ABOVE) and the anonymous Czech artist (LEFT) lived close to the site where the archetypal Earth Mother – The Venus of Willendorf – was found (see page 7).

———————◊———————

tion I had to get him to suck them they were so hard he said it was sweeter and thicker than cows then he wanted to milk me into the tea well hes beyond everything I declare somebody ought to put him in the budget if I only could remember the one half of the things and write a book out of it the works of Master Poldy yes and its so much smoother the skin much an hour he was at them Im sure by the clock like some kind of a big infant I had at me they want everything in their mouth all the pleasure those men get out of a woman I can feel his mouth O Lord I must stretch myself I wished he was here or somebody to let myself go with and come again like that I feel all fire inside me or if I could dream it when he made me spend the 2nd time tickling me behind with his finger I was coming for about 5 minutes with my legs around him I had to hug him after O Lord I wanted to shout out all sorts of things fuck or shit or anything at all only not to look ugly or those lines from the strain who knows the way hed take it you want to feel your way with a man theyre not all like him thank God some of them want you to be so nice about it I noticed the contrast he does it and doesnt talk I gave my eyes that look with my hair a bit loose from the tumbling and my tongue between my lips up to him the savage brute Thursday Friday one Saturday two Sunday three O Lord I cant wait till Monday

ABOVE One of a series of engravings made by the brilliant Belgian engraver Martin van Maele between 1905 and 1909.
OPPOSITE ABOVE An Indian ink drawing by Theo van Elsen who worked in Paris during the 1930s.

The last word on language and passion in erotic writing has to come from Henry Miller. Whatever the shortcomings of his later work, *Tropic of Cancer* and *Tropic of Capricorn* are powerful and unforgettable novels. In this extract it is not only the shocking images and words which are so remarkable, making a kind of surprising beauty out of ugliness, but the rhythm of the language, following one crescendo with another. The second part of the extract comes after the diatribe in the novel and is included because you may need a quiet walk on the Left Bank afterwards.

Tania is a fever, too – *les voies urinaires*, Café de la Liberté, Place des Vosges, bright neckties on the Boulevard Montparnasse, dark bathrooms, Porto Sec, Abdullah cigarettes, the adagio sonata *Pathétique*, aural amplificators, anecdotal seances, burnt sienna breasts, heavy garters, what time is it, golden pheasants stuffed with chestnuts, taffeta fingers, vaporish twilights turning to ilex, acromegaly, cancer and delirium, warm veils, poker chips, carpets of blood and soft thighs. Tania says so that every one may hear: 'I love him!' And while Boris scalds himself with whisky she

says: 'Sit down here! O Boris . . . *Russia* . . . what'll I do? I'm bursting with it!'

At night when I look at Boris' goatee lying on the pillow I get hysterical. O Tania, where now is that warm cunt of yours, those fat, heavy garters, those soft, bulging thighs? There is a bone in my prick six inches long. I will ream out every wrinkle in your cunt, Tania, big with seed. I will send you home to your Sylvester with an ache in your belly and your womb turned inside out. Your Sylvester! Yes, he knows how to build a fire, but I know how to inflame a cunt. I shoot hot bolts into you, Tania, I make your ovaries incandescent. Your Sylvester is a little jealous now? He feels something, does he? He feels the remnants of my big prick. I have set the shores a little wider, I have ironed out the wrinkles. After me you can take on stallions, bulls, rams, drakes, St. Bernards.

You can stuff toads, bats, lizards up your rectum. You can shit arpeggios if you like, or string a zither across your navel. I am fucking you, Tania, so that you'll stay fucked. And if you are afraid of being fucked publicly I will fuck you privately. I will tear off a few hairs from your cunt and paste them on Boris' chin. I will bite into your clitoris and spit out two franc pieces. . . .

ABOVE A woman pleasures her lover
'à l'espagnol' in this charcoal
drawing by A1.

Indigo sky swept clear of fleecy clouds, gaunt trees infinitely extended, their black boughs gesticulating like a sleepwalker. Somber, spectral trees, their trunks pale as cigar ash. A silence supreme and altogether European. Shutters drawn, shops barred. A red glow here and there to mark a tryst. Brusque the façades, almost forbidding; immaculate except for the splotches of shadow cast by the trees. Passing by the Orangerie I am reminded of another Paris, the Paris of Maugham, of Gauguin, Paris of George Moore. I think of that terrible Spaniard who was then startling the world with his acrobatic leaps from style to style. I think of Spengler and of his terrible pronunciamentos, and I wonder if style, style in the grand manner, is done for. I say that my mind is occupied with these thoughts, but it is not true; it is only later, after I have crossed the Seine, after I have put behind me the carnival of lights, that I allow my mind to play with these ideas. For the moment I can think of nothing – except that I am a sentient being stabbed by the miracle of these waters that reflect a forgotten world. All along the banks the trees lean heavily over the tarnished mirror; when the wind rises and fills them with a rustling murmur they will shed a few tears and shiver as the water swirls by. I am suffocated by it. No one to whom I can communicate even a fraction of my feelings. . . .

When the flames of passion die back to a steady glow, the great love manuals of the East encourage men and women to perfect a variety of sexual techniques that will keep boredom from the bedroom. At the conclusion of *Ananga-Ranga* ('State of the Bodiless One'), Kalyana Malla, who has an unsentimental view of human relationships, gives this advice:

The chief reason for the separation between the married couple and the cause, which drives the husband to the embraces of strange women, and the wife to the arms of strange men, is the want of varied pleasures and the monotony which follows possession. There is no doubt about it. Monotony begets satiety, and satiety distaste for congress, especially in one or the other; malicious feelings are engendered, the husband or the wife yields to temptation, and the other follows, being driven by jealousy. For it seldom happens that the two love each other equally, and in exact proportion, therefore is the one more easily seduced by passion than the other. From such separations result polygamy, adulteries, abortions, and every manner of vice, and not only do the erring husband and wife fall into the pit, but they also drag down the names of their deceased ancestors from the place of beautiful mortals, either to hell or back again upon this world. Fully understanding the way in which such quarrels arise, I have in this book shown how the husband, by varying the enjoyment of his wife, may live with her as with thirty-two different women, ever varying the enjoyment of her, and rendering satiety impossible.

The classical *Kama Sutra*, the love manuals of the Middle Ages (*Ananga-Ranga* and *Koka Shastra* notably) and numerous later Indian texts all teach that a variety of lovemaking positions is essential if the thrill and excitement of sex is to be maintained. These positions were given evocative names and described so that they could easily be learned by heart.

If you lift the girl by passing your elbows under her knees and enjoy her as she hangs trembling with her arms garlanding your neck, it is called *Janukurpura*, the Knee-Elbow.

If your lustful lover buries her face in the pillow and goes on all fours like an animal and you rut upon her from behind as though you were a wild beast, this coupling is *Harina*, the Deer.

When, straightening her legs, she grips and milks your penis with her vagina, as a mare holds a stallion, it is *Vadavaka*, the Mare, which is not learned without practice.

If, lying with her face turned away, the fawn-eyed girl offers you her buttocks and your penis enters the house of love, this is *Nagabandha*, the coupling of the Cobra.

LEFT For centuries the workshops of India produced erotic miniatures for the amusement of wealthy patrons and their ladies.

Caress my breasts with your fingers, they are small and you have neglected them. Enough! Now set your mouth just there immediately.

FROM THE SANSCRIT
AMARU, C. 800 AD

BELOW AND OPPOSITE Coloured woodcuts by Utamaro (1753–1806),
one of the greatest artists to work
in that medium.

Japanese erotic texts, in common with the Hindu love manuals, regard sex as a sacrament rather than a subject for
shame. 'The union of male and female, of man and woman,
symbolizes the union of the gods themselves at the moment when
the world was created. The gods smile upon your lovemaking,
enjoying your pleasure! For this reason both husband and wife
must strive to please each other and themselves when they

embrace. If you are both satisfied, the gods will be satisfied . . . good sex brings more honour to Daikoku than a well-tended altar.'

These words of wisdom come from the *Pillow Book*, written during the Kamakura period (1192–1333) by an aristocratic lady for the education of young women. It was the forerunner of many pillow books, all small and unillustrated since they were designed to be kept, together with combs and make-up, in the lacquered wood-

OPPOSITE BELOW A beautifully executed painting on fabric from the second half of the nineteenth century. Artist unknown.

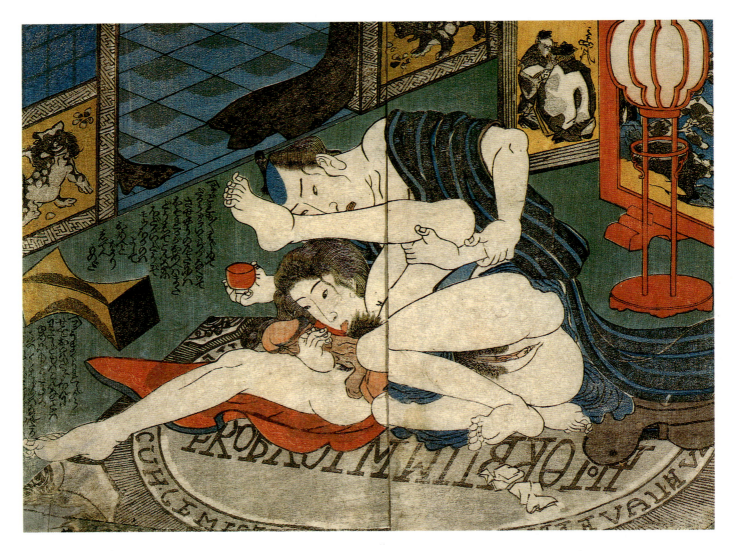

en pillow or *makura* which Japanese ladies slept on to preserve their elaborate coiffure.

The original *Pillow Book* was nothing if not direct: all problems were attacked with the same attention to detail. Homosexuality was common among the samurai (as in many elite fighting brotherhoods: the Sacred Bands of ancient Greece; the imperial Turkish Janissaries; Oliver Cromwell's Model Army) and if the relationship with a husband whose tastes tended that way were to be preserved, 'the young wife should offer him her anus from time to time. She should pay scrupulous attention to hygiene and prepare herself carefully with lubricating cream.'

The *Pillow Book* offered psychological as well as physical advice. Newly married wives are told to find subtle ways of praising their husband's penis. When it is flaccid, sly comments such as 'how huge your penis is, my love, so much larger than I remember my father's when he went naked to the bath-house' are suggested. In erection she should try, 'I cannot believe how big your penis is, my love. Is it possible that I can accommodate such a wonder? Fill me now!' Lastly, this inspired medieval sex counsellor exhorts women to miss no opportunity of telling their husbands 'how manly you are, how fortunate I am to have such a man!'

Although the *Pillow Book* and most of its later imitators were unillustrated (or at best poorly illustrated), Japan did produce some of the most extraordinary erotic art the world has ever seen – shunga. Early shunga prints were often commissioned by the owners of the great bordellos or 'green houses' as advertisements. One set from 1660 shows forty-eight different sexual positions, almost rivalling the Hindu tradition in imagination. When he saw shunga prints for the first time, the nineteenth-century French writer Edmond de Goncourt was clearly both shocked and excited: 'The animal frenzies of the flesh . . . the fury of copulation as if transported by rage!'

Shunga was the art of 'the floating world' or the 'city without night'. This referred to the pleasure districts of Japan's great cities, where in the eighteenth and nineteenth centuries every kind of aesthetic and sensual delight was available. Here, poets and artists lived side by side with the cultured and refined courte-

Shunga prints by Koriusai (OPPOSITE) and from a pillow book (LEFT).

sans of the 'green houses'. These were greenhouses indeed, steamy hotbeds of political and cultural radicalism where masters of the four-colour woodblock print like Harunobu, Utamaro and Hokusai created unforgettable and often very amusing erotic images. Shunga prints are the fireworks of erotic art: penises enlarged to erupting roman candles, vulvas like catherine wheels, the image alive with movement and vibrant with colour and pattern.

In China the 'refinement of passion' finds expression in the elaborate symbolism of Taoism. In the religious text known as *I Ching* ('The Book of Changes') dating from around 1200 BC, Tao (the whole, perfection, cosmic order) is shown to come from the interaction of Yin (male) and Yang (female). This interaction occurs in all things. The sky is Yin, the earth is Yang; mountains are Yin, valleys Yang, and so on. In this sexualized cosmos it follows that lovemaking is central: the *I Ching* goes so far as to say that 'the sexual union of man and woman gives life to all things'.

Taoist sages produced love manuals at a very early date. Centuries later these texts formed the basis for the Japanese tradition of erotology. The Taoist manuals gave evocative names to the various lovemaking positions such as 'Galloping Horse' and 'Monkey Facing Tree'. Successive waves of censorship under Confucianism have meant that visual erotic art in China, even at its best, cannot compare with Japanese or Indian erotic art: the principles of proportion and subtleties of anatomy were never mastered by Chinese artists. Instead, eroticism found expression in the symbolism of landscape painting and in the great erotic novels of the Ming Period such as *Chin P'ing Mei* ('Metal Vase Plum Blossom'). In both art forms we need to understand the symbolism in order to release the erotic meaning. The title of *Chin P'ing Mei* contains 'vase', a female symbol, and 'plum', a male one: if this subtlety is lost we miss the whole point of Chinese erotic writing (see also the poems of Ikkyu on page 55). However, given this key, we begin to understand that the *Chin P'ing Mei* is like an erotic concerto.

Pear Blossom poured wine for Lady Ping and her guest, Hsi-Men, and left the pair to their guilty pleasures. Believing themselves alone, how quickly the lovers undressed one another with urgent fingers and gasps of pleasure: he at the scented arbors of her armpits and belly and the secret fruits ripe and luscious. She at the jade stalk risen up and the heavy purse of pleasure. But what is this? Pear Blossom the sly one has made a hole in the paper of the wall so that she can spy upon the lovers at their games. This shameless girl is near enough to feel the gusts of breath from her mistress as he opens the scented field of cinnabar with his

BELOW A Chinese nineteenth-century rosewood toilet box with eleven concealed miniatures.

tongue. The maid is so close she can even hear the music of the jade flute as it slips over the tongue and lips of her mistress.

What wild scene is this? Now the glistening gateway of jade is offered to him, and the leaping white tiger crosses the fields of snow. The pace is furious now and the lovers call out to each other, Mistress Ping noisy from both mouths as the purple plum moves between her lips. She turns to spur on the rider, her heavy hair dancing about her temples. And who can remain dry in such a storm as this? Pear Blossom's own cup is full and her fingers dance in the moisture.

All are lost now. Hsi-Men shouts as his fire juices spurt, Lady Ping moans as the thunder shakes her thighs and outside in the cold a little one shudders.

In ancient China, novel writing was not regarded as a worthy occupation for a serious man of letters and none of the time-honoured literary conventions applied. For this reason much of *Chin P'ing Mei* was written in a spare colloquial style, perfectly captured in the scholarly and accurate translation by Clement Egerton. This version, published in 1939, was entitled *The Golden Lotus* and the numerous sexual descriptions (for example, of fellatio in this extract) had to be rendered in Latin to avoid prosecution.

Hsi-mên Ch'ing and his ladies made merry in the Hibiscus Arbour. They drank till it was late, and then went to their own apartments. Hsi-mên Ch'ing went to Golden Lotus's room. He was already half drunk, and soon wished to enjoy the delights of love with his new lady. Golden Lotus hastily burned incense, and they took off their clothes and went to bed. But Hsi-mên Ch'ing would not allow her to go too fast. He knew that she played the flute exquisitely. He sat down behind the curtains of the bed, and set her before him. Then Golden Lotus daintily pushed back the golden bracelets from her wrists and *mentulam ad sua labra adposuit* [brought his jade stalk to her lips], while he leaned forward to enjoy the delight of her movements. She continued for a long time, and all the while his delight grew greater. He called Plum Blossom to bring in some tea. Golden Lotus was afraid that her maid would see her, and hastily pulled down the bed curtains.

ABOVE A painting on silk, c. 1730.

Last night a peach petal was wetted by
the rain,
And when a girl
After her toilet said:
'Which is the more beautiful,
I or the peach petal?'
And he said:
'Peach petal wetted by the rain is
incomparable,'
There were tears and a tearing of
flowers.

To taste the living flower
Tonight would be quite a good night,
my lord,
If so you wish.

DEAD FLOWER, OR LIVING?
GEISHA SONG, LATE EIGHTEENTH CENTURY

RIGHT Confucian restrictions
meant that Chinese artists were
never really allowed to master
either perspective or anatomy.
This painting was executed on silk.

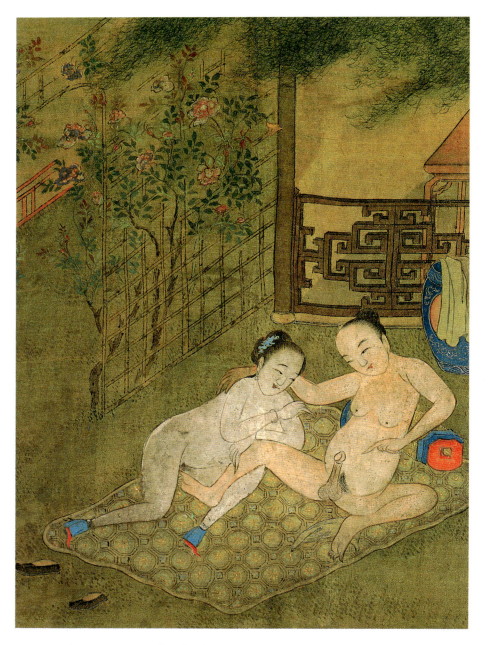

'What are you afraid of?' Hsi-mên said. 'Our neighbour Hua
has two excellent maids. One of them, the younger, brought us
those flowers to-day, but there is another about as old as Plum
Blossom. Brother Hua has already taken her virginity. Indeed
wherever her mistress is, she is too. She is really very pretty, and
of course no one can tell what a man like Brother Hua may do in
the privacy of his own home.'

Golden Lotus looked at him.

'You are a strange creature, but I will not scold you,' she said.
'If you wish to have this girl, have her and be done with it. Why
go beating about the bush, pointing at a mountain when you
really are thinking about something quite different. I know you

would like to have somebody else to compare with me, but I am not jealous. She is not actually my maid. To-morrow, I will go to the garden to rest for a while, and that will give you a chance. You can call her into this room and do what you like with her. Will that satisfy you?'

Hsi-mên Ch'ing was delighted. 'You understand me so well!' he said, 'how can I help loving you?' So these two agreed, and their delight in each other and in their love could not have been greater. After she had played the flute, they kissed each other, and went to sleep.

The next day Golden Lotus went to the apartments of Tower of Jade, and Hsi-mên Ch'ing called Plum Blossom to his room, and had his pleasure of her.

From that day, Golden Lotus showered favours on this girl. She would not allow her to go and wait at the kitchen, but kept her to attend to her bedroom, and serve her with tea. She chose beautiful clothes and ornaments for her, and bound her feet very tightly.

LEFT A small ivory carving of lovers, dating from the nineteenth century.

Erotic symbolism was used with powerful effect in the poetry of the Semitic peoples. The *Song of Songs* in the Bible, attributed to King Solomon but in reality a Lebanese marriage song from a later period, is a marvellous example. These are some fragments. Read it in its entirety in the Bible; it is one of the great erotic poems of the world.

THE SHULAMITE

Let him kiss me with the kisses of his mouth:
For thy love is better than wine.
Thine ointments have a goodly fragrance;
Thy name is as ointment poured forth;
Therefore do the virgins love thee.

THE DAUGHTERS OF JERUSALEM

We will be glad and rejoice in thee,
We will make mention of thy love more than of wine:
Rightly do they love thee.

THE SHULAMITE

I am black, but comely,
O ye daughters of Jerusalem,
As the tents of Kedar,
As the curtains of Solomon.
Look not upon me, because I am swarthy,
Because the sun hath scorched me.

KING SOLOMON

I have compared thee, O my love,
To a steed in Pharaoh's chariots.
Thy cheeks are comely with plaits of hair,
Thy neck with strings of jewels.
We will make thee plaits of gold
With studs of silver.

THE SHULAMITE

While the king sat at his table,
My spikenard sent forth its fragrance.
My beloved is unto me as a bundle of myrrh,
That lieth betwixt my breasts.
My beloved is unto me as a cluster of henna-flowers
In the vineyards of En-gedi.

KING SOLOMON

Behold, thou art fair, my love; behold, thou art fair;
Thine eyes are as doves.

THE SHULAMITE

Behold, thou art fair, my beloved, yea, pleasant;
Also our couch is green.
The beams of our house are cedars,
And our rafters are firs.

I am a rose of Sharon,
A lily of the valleys.

KING SOLOMON

As a lily among thorns,
So is my love among the daughters.

THE SHULAMITE

As the apple tree among the trees of the wood,
So is my beloved among the sons.
I sat down under his shadow with great delight,
And his fruit was sweet to my taste.

He brought me to the banqueting house,
And his banner over me was love.
Stay ye me with raisins, comfort me with apples:
For I am sick of love.
His left hand is under my head,
And his right hand doth embrace me.

I adjure you, O daughters of Jerusalem,
By the roes, and by the hinds of the field,
That ye stir not up, nor awaken love,
Until it please.

THE SHULAMITE

My beloved is mine, and I am his:
He feedeth his flock among the lilies.
Until the day be cool, and the shadows flee away,
Turn, my beloved, and be thou like a roe or a young hart
Upon the mountains of Bether.

. . . By night on my bed I sought him whom my soul
    loveth:
I sought him, but I found him not.
I said, 'I will rise now, and go about the city,
In the streets and in the broad ways,
I will seek him whom my soul loveth':
I sought him, but I found him not.

The watchmen that go about the city found me:
To whom I said, 'Saw ye him whom my soul loveth?'
It was but a little that I passed from them,
When I found him whom my soul loveth:
I held him, and would not let him go,

Until I had brought him into my mother's house,
And into the chamber of her that conceived me.

THE DAUGHTERS OF JERUSALEM

Who is this that cometh up out of the wilderness like
  pillars of smoke,
Perfumed with myrrh and frankincense,
With all powders of the merchant?

KING SOLOMON

Behold thou art fair, my love; behold, thou art fair;
Thine eyes are as doves behind thy veil:
Thy hair is as a flock of goats,
That lie along the side of Mount Gilead.

Thy teeth are like a flock of ewes that are newly shorn,
Which are come up from the washing;
Whereof every one hath twins,
And none is bereaved among them.

Thy lips are like a thread of scarlet,
And thy mouth is comely:
Thy temples are like a piece of a pomegranate
Behind thy veil.
Thy neck is like the tower of David builded for an
  armoury,
Whereon there hang a thousand bucklers,
All the shields of the mighty men.
Thy two breasts are like two fawns that are twins of a
  roe,
Which feed among the lilies.

Until the day be cool, and the shadows flee away,
I will get me to the mountain of myrrh,
And to the hill of frankincense.

Thou art all fair, my love;
And there is no spot in thee.
Come with me from Lebanon, my bride,
With me from Lebanon:
Look from the top of Amana.

KING SOLOMON

How beautiful are thy feet in sandals, O prince's
  daughter!
The joints of thy thighs are like jewels,
The work of the hands of a cunning workman.
Thy navel is like a round goblet,
Wherein no mingled wine is wanting:
Thy belly is like a heap of wheat
Set about with lilies.

Thy two breasts are like two fawns
That are twins of a roe.

Thy neck is like the tower of ivory;
Thine eyes as the pools in Heshbon, by the gate of
  Bath-rabbim;
Thy nose is like the tower of Lebanon
Which looketh toward Damascus.

Thine head upon thee is like Carmel,
And the hair of thine head like purple;
The king is held captive in the tresses thereof.
How fair and how pleasant art thou,
O love, for delights!
This thy stature is like to a palm tree,
And thy breasts to clusters of grapes.

I said, 'I will climb up into the palm tree,
I will take hold of the branches thereof':
Let thy breasts be as clusters of the vine,
And the smell of thy breath like apples;
And thy mouth like the best wine,
That goeth down smoothly for my beloved,
Gliding through the lips of those that are asleep.

THE SHULAMITE

I am my beloved's,
And his desire is toward me.
Come, my beloved, let us go forth into the field;
Let us lodge in the villages.
Let us get up early to the vineyards;
Let us see whether the vine hath budded, and its
  blossom be open,
And the pomegranates be in flower:

There will I give thee my love.
The mandrakes give forth fragrance,
And at our doors are all manner of precious fruits,
  new and old,
Which I have laid up for thee, O my beloved.

Oh that thou wert as my brother,
That sucked the breasts of my mother!
When I should find thee without, I would kiss thee;
Yea, and none would despise me.

I would lead thee, and bring thee into my mother's
  house,
Who would instruct me;
I would cause thee to drink of spiced wine,
Of the juice of my pomegranate.
His left hand should be under my head,
And his right hand should embrace me.

I adjure you, O daughters of Jerusalem,
That ye stir not up, nor awaken love,
Until it please.

The Islamic world is rich in erotic literature, from the wonders of Persian poetry to the dazzling collection of stories known as *The Arabian Nights*. There have been numerous translations of the *Nights* into Western languages but Sir Richard Burton's version is incomparable. Burton was sympathetic towards Arab culture and managed to capture the rhythm of the poetry in English: 'She hath breasts like two globes of ivory, like golden pomegranates, beautifully upright, arched and rounded, firm as stone to the touch, with nipples erect and outward jutting. She hath thighs like unto pillars of alabaster, and between them, there vaunts a secret place, a sachet of musk, that swells, that throbs, that is moist and avid.'

Sir Richard Burton also translated the most famous of the Arab love manuals, *The Perfumed Garden* of Sheikh Nefzawi. When he died he had just completed a revised version which included the missing chapter on homosexual practices. Unfortunately this was burned by Isabel, his wife, in one of the most notorious bonfires in literary history. Homosexual incidents feature in *The Arabian Nights*, and many of the Arab sex manuals give advice on the subject. *The Book of Counsel* of the eleventh-century Emir Kai-Ka'us ibn Iskander recommends, mysteriously, that the reader should 'in summer devote himself to boys, in winter to women'.

The Perfumed Garden is an urbane, worldly-wise book, full of wicked humour and very different in tone from the Hindu love manuals. The author – writing to ingratiate himself with the Grand Vizier of Tunis but not above slyly sending up his patron – admits that the Hindus had more lovemaking positions but enumerates what he judges the basic ones. He begins with foreplay.

Concerning all that is Favourable to Coition

Know, oh Vizier, (God's mercy be with you!) that if you wish to experience an agreeable copulation, one that gives equal satisfaction and pleasure to both parties, it is necessary to frolic with the woman and excite her with nibbling, kissing, and caressing. Turn her over on the bed, sometimes on her back, sometimes on her belly, until you see by her eyes that the moment of pleasure has arrived, as I have described in the previous chapter, and, on my honour! I have not stinted the descriptions.

When, therefore, you see a woman's lips tremble and redden, and her eyes become languishing and her sighs profound, know that she desires coition; then is the time to get between her thighs and penetrate her. If you have followed my advice you will both enjoy a delightful copulation which will leave a delicious memory. Someone has said: 'If you desire to copulate, place the woman on the ground, embrace her closely and put your lips on hers; then clasp her, suck her, bite her; kiss her neck, her breasts, her belly and her flanks; strain her to you until she lies limp with desire. When you see her in this state, introduce your member. If you act thus your enjoyment will be simultaneous, and that is the secret of pleasure. But if you neglect this plan the woman will not satisfy your desires, and she herself will gain no enjoyment.'

ABOVE Fragment of a hand-written, illuminated love manual.

——— CONCERNING THE DIFFERENT POSTURES FOR COITION ———
The ways of uniting with a woman are numerous and varied, and
the time has arrived when you should learn the different postures. . . .

According to your taste you may choose the posture which
pleases you most, provided always that intercourse takes place
through the appointed organ: the vulva.

BELOW An Arabian Nights scene of
lovers enjoying one another on a
Persian carpet under the stars.

FIRST POSTURE Lay the woman on her back and raise her thighs; then, getting between her legs, introduce your member. Gripping the ground with your toes, you will be able to move in a suitable manner. This posture is a good one for those who have long members.

SECOND POSTURE If your member is short, lay the woman on her back and raise her legs in the air so that her toes touch her ears. Her buttocks being thus raised, the vulva is thrown forward. Now introduce your member.

THIRD POSTURE Lay the woman on the ground and get between her thighs; then, putting one of her legs on your shoulder and the other under your arm, penetrate her.

FOURTH POSTURE Stretch the woman on the ground and put her legs on your shoulders; in that position your member will be exactly opposite her vulva which will be lifted off the ground. That is the moment for introducing your member.

FIFTH POSTURE Let the woman lie on her side on the ground; then, lying down yourself and getting between her thighs, introduce your member. This posture is apt to give rise to rheumatic or sciatic pains.

SIXTH POSTURE Let the woman rest on her knees and elbows in the position for prayer. In this posture the vulva stands out behind. Attack her thus.

SEVENTH POSTURE Lay the woman on her side, and then you yourself sitting on your heels will place her top leg on your nearest shoulder and her other leg against your thighs. She will keep on her side and you will be between her legs. Introduce your member and move her backwards and forwards with your hands.

EIGHTH POSTURE Lay the woman on her back and kneel astride her.

NINTH POSTURE Place the woman so that she rests, either face forward or the reverse, against a slightly raised platform, her feet remaining on the ground and her body projecting in front. She will thus present her vulva to your member which you will introduce.

TENTH POSTURE Place the woman on a rather low divan and let her grasp the woodwork with her hands; then, placing her legs on your hips and telling her to grip your body with them, you will introduce your member, at the same time grasping the divan. When you begin to work, let your movements keep time.

ELEVENTH POSTURE Lay the woman on her back and let her buttocks be raised by a cushion placed under them. Let her put the soles of her feet together: now get between her thighs.

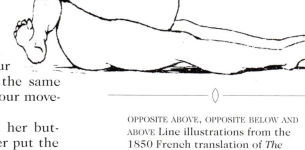

OPPOSITE ABOVE, OPPOSITE BELOW AND ABOVE Line illustrations from the 1850 French translation of *The Perfumed Garden*.

Roman writers discussed different sexual positions, but there is none of the subtlety and insight of Hindu commentators and little concern for the feelings of the woman. The best of them was Ovid, whose *Ars Amatoria* ('The Art of Love'), written at the time of Christ, does at least address itself to women as well as to men: 'Reckon up each of your charms, and take your posture according to your beauty. One and the same mode does not become every woman. If you are especially attractive of face – lie on your back . . . Let her press the bed with her knees, the neck slightly bowed, she whose chief beauty is her shapely flank . . . '

Rear-entry lovemaking, 'the posterior Venus', and the position known as 'the horse of Hector' where the woman rides the man, seem to have been especially popular in Classical times. They may seem plain fare compared with the infinite possibilities offered by Eastern authorities, but in our culture they have stood the test of time. To end this section on the refinements of passion we will follow these two basic sexual postures, or motifs, down through the ages.

Aristophanes, the great Greek comic dramatist writing in the fifth to fourth centuries BC, refers to rear-entry lovemaking both in *The Peace* and in *Lysistrata*, the heroine of which complains: 'I will not squat on all fours like a lioness!' Athenaeus, writing in the second century AD, makes it clear that the 'posterior Venus' was still popular throughout the Greek world. He records that a famous courtesan allowed herself to be mounted five times in succession in that, her favourite, posture by a dirty but handsome travelling

The sun begins to bleed
On the spikes of the palm trees
and now he falls
a bursting crimson pomegranate
from all the branches;
your mat is the world tonight
and you are the sun setting
and I am the darkness
coming down over you.

HER SONG
FRAGMENTARY POEM FROM FRENCH
INDO-CHINA, NINETEENTH CENTURY

tinker who caught her eye. News of this reached the market place and when she was reproached by her protector she made the ingenious excuse that she could not possibly have allowed such a dirty, low-born rogue to touch her breasts and make them sooty!

The beauty of female buttocks was so admired by the Greeks that they held public competitions in which girls revealed their 'derrières' to a panel of judges. Athenaeus tells the story of two sisters who lived near Syracuse who had often won prizes for their magnificent behinds, but quarrelled over whose was the most splendid. To resolve matters they exposed themselves simultaneously to an unsuspecting youth on the highway (thus anticipating 'mooning' by 2,000 years). He fell for the elder sister (or rather her bottom) and married her, but not before his younger brother had decided to make it a double ceremony. The chronicler records that the sisters were known by the inhabitants of Syracuse as Callipygi because, although of lowly birth, their posteriors served them for a dowry. Full of gratitude, the newly rich sisters dedicated a temple to Venus, under the title of Venus Callipygos (Venus of the beauteous buttocks).

The Romans were no less fond of the 'posterior Venus' and the well-preserved frescoes of the Pompeii brothel show that it was one of the main attractions of the establishment. After the fall of the Roman empire the practice evidently did not go out of fashion, because at the dawning of the Renaissance Boccaccio is able to tell this delightful bawdy tale (or tail) in which the artful priest Dom Gianni contrives to enjoy Gossip Pietro's buxom wife Gemmata in his favourite manner.

Gossip Pietro on his part, albeit he was very poor and had but a little cot at Tresanti that scarce sufficed for himself, his fair, young wife, and their ass, nevertheless, whenever Dom Gianni arrived at Tresanti, made him welcome, and did him the honours of his house as best he might, in requital of the hospitality which he received at Barletta. However, as Gossip Pietro had but one little bed, in which he slept with his fair wife, 'twas not in his power to lodge Dom Gianni as comfortably as he would have liked; but the priest's mare being quartered beside the ass in a little stable, the priest himself must needs lie beside her on the straw. Many a time when the priest came, the wife, knowing how honourably he entreated her husband at Barletta, would fain have gone to sleep with a neighbour, one Zita Carapresa di Giudice Leo, that the priest might share the bed with her husband, and many a time had she told the priest so: howbeit he would never agree to it, and on one occasion: – 'Gossip Gemmata,' quoth he, 'trouble not thyself about me; I am well lodged; for, when I am so minded, I turn the mare into a fine lass and dally with her, and then, when I would, I turn her back into a mare; wherefore I could ill brook to part from her.' The young woman, wondering but believing, told her husband what the priest had said, adding: – 'If he is even such a friend as thou sayst, why dost thou not get him to teach thee the enchantment, so that thou mayst turn me into a mare,

ABOVE A pencil drawing by an anonymous Italian artist who was active in the 1880s.

*There on the vulgar on the humble bed
I had the body of love, I had the lips,
The sensuous, the rosy lips of wine,
Rosy with such a wine, that even now
Here as I write, after so many years,
In my solitary house, I am drunk
    again.*

FROM *ONE NIGHT*
C. P. CAVAFY (1863–1933)

LEFT *An Offering to the God
Priapus*, painted by an unknown
French artist at the end of the
eighteenth century.

and have both ass and mare for thine occasions? We should then make twice as much gain as we do, and thou couldst turn me back into a woman when we came home at night.'

Gossip Pietro, whose wit was somewhat blunt, believed that 'twas as she said, approved her counsel, and began adjuring Dom Gianni, as persuasively as he might, to teach him the incantation. Dom Gianni did his best to wean him of his folly; but as all was in vain: – 'Lo, now,' quoth he, 'as you are both bent on it, we will be up, as is our wont, before the sun to-morrow morning, and I will shew you how 'tis done. The truth is that 'tis in the attachment of the tail that the great difficulty lies, as thou wilt see.' Scarce a wink of sleep had either Gossip Pietro or Gossip Gemmata that night, so great was their anxiety; and towards daybreak up they got, and called Dom Gianni; who, being risen, came in

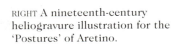

RIGHT A nineteenth-century heliogravure illustration for the 'Postures' of Aretino.

his shirt into Gossip Pietro's little bedroom, and: – 'I know not,' quoth he, 'that there is another soul in the world for whom I would do this, save you, my gossips; however, as you will have it so, I will do it, but it behoves you to do exactly as I bid you, if you would have the enchantment work.' They promised obedience, and Dom Gianni thereupon took a light, which he handed to Gossip Pietro, saying: – 'Let nought that I shall do or say escape thee; and have a care, so thou wouldst not ruin all, to say never a word, whatever thou mayst see or hear; and pray God that the tail may be securely attached.' So Gossip Pietro took the light, and again promised obedience; Dom Gianni caused Gossip Gemmata to strip herself stark naked, and stand on all fours like a mare, at the same time strictly charging her that, whatever might happen,

LEFT A drawing by the highly gifted German artist and illustrator Franz von Bayros (1866–1924). Clearly influenced by Beardsley and the Decadents, von Bayros – whose work was almost exclusively erotic – was obliged to move from one European capital to another as each outrageous new work was banned by the authorities.
BELOW An illustration from a French erotic manual published during the Age of Enlightenment.

she must utter no word. Then, touching her head and face: – 'Be this a fine head of a mare,' quoth he; in like manner touching her hair, he said: – 'Be this a fine mane of a mare;' touching her arms: – 'Be these fine legs and fine hooves of a mare;' then, as he touched her breast and felt its firm roundness, and there awoke

BELOW Further illustrations from the erotic manual also shown at right on page 105.

BACCHUS ET ARIANE.

LA MUSIQUE EN DÉLIRE.

JULIE AVEC UN ATHLETE.

and arose one that was not called: – 'And be this a fine breast of a mare,' quoth he; and in like manner he dealt with her back, belly, croup, thighs, and legs. Last of all, the work being complete save for the tail, he lifted his shirt and took in his hand the tool with which he was used to plant men, and forthwith thrust it into the furrow made for it, saying: – 'And be this a fine tail of a mare.' Whereat Gossip Pietro, who had followed everything very heedfully to that point, disapproving that last particular, exclaimed: – 'No! Dom Gianni, I'll have no tail, I'll have no tail.' The essential juice, by which all plants are propagated, was already discharged, when Dom Gianni withdrew the tool, saying: – 'Alas! Gossip Pietro, what hast thou done? Did I not tell thee to say never a word, no matter what thou mightst see? The mare was all but made; but by speaking thou hast spoiled all; and 'tis not possible to repeat the enchantment.' 'Well and good,' replied Gossip Pietro, 'I would have none of that tail. Why saidst thou not to me: – "Make it thou"? And besides, thou wast attaching it too low.' ''Twas because,' returned Dom Gianni, 'thou wouldst not have known, on the first essay, how to attach it so well as I.' Whereupon the young woman stood up, and in all good faith said to her husband: – 'Fool that thou art, wherefore hast thou brought to nought what had been for the good of us both? When didst thou ever see mare without a tail? So help me God, poor as thou art, thou deservest to be poorer still.' So, after Gossip Pietro's ill-timed speech, there being no way left of returning the young woman into a mare, downcast and melancholy she resumed her clothes; and Gossip Pietro plied his old trade with his ass, and went with Dom Gianni to the fair of Bitonto, and never asked him so to serve him again.

Three hundred years after Boccaccio wrote the *Decameron*, the young French lawyer Nicolas Chorier put his Classical education to an unexpected use when he wrote *Satyra Sotadica* in impeccable Latin. In this vigorous translation of the original it is Fabrizio who takes up the baton in our erotic relay race.

Fabrizio makes ready for another attack. His member is swollen up, red and threatening. 'I beg of you Madam', he says, 'turn over on your face.' I did as he wished. When he saw my buttocks, whiter than ivory and snow, 'How beautiful you are!' he cried. 'But raise yourself on your knees, and bend your head down.' I bow my head and bosom, and lift my buttocks. He thrust his swift-moving and fiery dart to the bottom of my vulva, and took one of my nipples in either hand. Then he began to work in and out, and soon sent a sweet rivulet into the cavity of Venus. I also felt unspeakable delight, and had nearly fainted with lust. A surprising quantity of seed secreted by Fabrizio's loins filled and delighted me; a similar flow of my own exhausted my forces.

Where Fanny Hill describes the same 'mode of enjoyment' in 1749, some sixty years later, it seems to have become slightly more

unusual (two incidents in a book full of incident). This is not because the author John Cleland was provincial – he had travelled widely in Europe and India. Whether this indicates personal taste or contemporary manners is not clear. One of the charms of this passage, incidentally, is the emphasis on respect for the young ladies of the establishment, in marked contrast to the tone of much of the so-called erotic material available today.

> Her spark then endeavoured, as she stood, by disclosing her thighs, to gain us a completer sight of that central charm of attraction, but not obtaining it so conveniently in that attitude, he led her to the foot of the couch, and bringing to it one of the pillows, gently inclin'd her head down, so that as she leaned with it over her crossed hands, straddling with her thighs wide spread, and jutting her body out, she presented a full back view of her person, naked to her waist. Her posteriors, plump, smooth, and prominent, form'd luxuriant tracts of animated snow, that splendidly filled the eye, till it was commanded down the parting or separation of those exquisitely white cliffs, by their narrow vale, and was there stopt, and attracted by the embowered bottom-cavity that terminated this delightful vista and stood moderately

ABOVE Thomas Rowlandson produced the majority of his erotic works towards the end of his life when debauchery had already taken its toll of his health and quite possibly his virility as well. Prints like this are as much a joke against himself as against the voyeuristic perversities of old rakes in general.

ABOVE An eighteenth-century
French engraving.

gaping from the influence of her bended posture, so that the
agreeable interior red of the sides of the orifice came into
view, and with respect to the white that dazzled round it,
gave somewhat the idea of a pink slash in the glossi-
est white satin. Her gallant, who was a gentleman
about thirty, somewhat inclin'd to a fatness that
was in no sort displeasing, improving the hint thus
tendered him of this mode of enjoyment, after
settling her well in this posture, and encouraging
her with kisses and caresses to stand him
through, drew out his affair ready erected, and
whose extreme length, rather disproportion'd to
its breadth, was the more surprising, as that excess
is not often the case with those of his corpulent
habit; making then the right and direct application,
he drove it up to the guard, whilst the round bulge of
those Turkish beauties of hers tallying with the hollow
made with the bent of his belly and thighs, as they curved
inwards, brought all those parts, surely not undelightfully, into
warm touch, and close conjunction; his hands he kept passing
round her body, and employed in toying with her enchanting
breasts. As soon too as she felt him at home as he could reach,
she lifted her head a little from the pillow, and turning her neck,
without much straining, but her cheeks glowing with the deepest
scarlet, and a smile of the tenderest satisfaction, met the kiss he
press'd forward to give her as they were thus close joined together: when leaving him to pursue his delights, she hid again her
face and blushes with her hands and pillow, and thus stood pas-
sively and as favourably too as she could, whilst he kept laying at
her with repeated thrusts and making the meeting flesh on both
sides resound again with the violence of them; then ever as he
backen'd from her, we could see between them part of his long
white staff foamingly in motion, till, as he went on again and
closed with her, the interposing hillocks took it out of sight.
Sometimes he took his hands from the semi-globes of her bosom,
and transferred the pressure of them to those larger ones, the
present subjects of his soft blockade, which he squeez'd, grasp'd,
and play'd with, till at length a pursuit of driving, so hotly urged,
brought on the height of the fit with such overpowering pleasure
that his fair partner became now necessary to support him, panting, fainting, and dying as he discharged; which she no sooner
felt the killing sweetness of than, unable to keep her legs, and
yielding to the mighty intoxication, she reeled, and falling forward on the couch, made it a necessity for him, if he would preserve the warm pleasure-hold, to fall upon her, where they
perfected, in a continued conjunction of body and ecstatic flow,
their scheme of joys for that time.

As soon as he had disengag'd, the charming Emily got up, and
we crowded round her with congratulations and other officious
little services; for it is to be noted, that though all modesty and
reserve were banished from the transaction of these pleasures,
good manners and politeness were inviolably observ'd: here was
no gross ribaldry, no offensive or rude behaviour, or ungenerous

Gods! that a thing admired by me
Should fall to so much infamy.
Had she picked out, to rub her arse on,
Some stiff-pricked clown or well-hung
parson,
Each job of whose spermatic sluice
Had filled her cunt with wholesome
juice,
I the proceeding should have praised
In hope sh'had quenched a fire I
raised.
Such natural freedoms are but just:
There's something generous in mere
lust.

FROM *A RAMBLE IN ST JAMES'S PARK*
JOHN WILMOT, EARL OF ROCHESTER
(1647–80)

reproaches to the girls for their compliance with the humours and desires of the men; on the contrary, nothing was wanting to soothe, encourage, and soften the sense of their condition to them. Men know not in general how much they destroy of their own pleasure, when they break through the respect and tenderness due to our sex, and even to those of it who live only by pleasing them. And this was a maxim perfectly well understood by these polite voluptuaries, these profound adepts in the great art and science of pleasure, who never shew'd these votaries of theirs a more tender respect than at the time of those exercises of their complaisance, when they unlock'd their treasures of concealed beauty, and showed out in the pride of their native charms, evermore touching surely than when they parade it in the artificial ones of dress and ornament.

———◇———

The last example of this lovemaking position is taken from *The Boudoir*, published during the High Victorian age when even the primmest lady pinched in her waist with a corset and wore a bustle to emphasize her behind. It comes as no surprise that the 'posterior Venus' was also fashionable in the best quality erotic magazine of the period.

———◇———

ABOVE An illustration by Antoine Borel (1743–1810).
BELOW LEFT The first of three erotic drawings (see overleaf) by the Hungarian painter Mihály Zichy.

———◇———

Suddenly, I heard a noise in the passage. I rose with a bound, rushed to the door, and looked through the keyhole. If it was my husband, we were lost. Happily, I was mistaken.

I sighed to F. that there was naught to fear. In this position, with my eye fixed to the lock, my buttocks were exposed, and my shift was all tucked up. In a twinkling, my lover was behind me, and before I had time to collect myself I was penetrated again,

ABOVE AND OPPOSITE Mihály Zichy (1827–1906) worked in Budapest, Vienna and Paris, and was successively Court Painter at St Petersburg and in Moscow for Czar Alexander II. It was not a happy life and even the most erotic of his superb drawings have a melancholy air.

filled up by that adorable instrument that seemed to know no rest. Ah! How I helped him by opening and shutting the cheeks of my backside . . . by writhing, twisting, and swooning with joy.

Our time had passed quickly. In haste, I sent away my lover, made the bed afresh, and arranged a neat toilette for the promenade. I was scarcely ready when the carriage drove up, and my husband came to fetch me. He found me flushed and lively, I answered that, overcome by the heat, I had fallen asleep.

We went downstairs, and I was joyfully saluted by the gentlemen, who complimented me on the novelty and good taste of my costume. On the sly, I looked at F., but nothing happily betrayed that anything extraordinary had taken place. We started off.

The forest we were exploring was deliciously cool and picturesque; we went to the lodge of a game-keeper, where a slight rustic repast had been prepared. Our collation was merrily enjoyed, I was forced to drink several glasses of champagne, although I did not require that to stimulate me.

After the meal we set out walking again, my husband gossiped with F. I was with them. The two guests had strolled into another path when we arrived at a wild spot, studded with rocks, and shaded with large trees.

At this moment one of the gentlemen, who were far off, called out to my husband: 'Come, quick, come and see!'

Charles ran away and left us. Directly he had disappeared from view, F. glued his mouth to mine.

'Angel,' said he, 'let us profit by this moment!'

'You are mad!'

'No, I love you, let me do as I will.'

'My God, we shall be discovered! I am lost!'

'Not if you hurry. Stoop!'

'Are you in?'

'Here I am. It's going in!'

'Ah! make haste. I tremble!'

'There, darling . . . spend . . . spend again!'

'Ah! I've come! Now go away.'

'Oh! Go.'

Only just in time. My petticoats, all up behind, were barely readjusted, when I heard the rest of the party returning.

I went to meet them, and we found they had fetched us to see a swarm of bees captured from the top of a tree.

We got into our carriages and returned to the town. We danced at night at the Pump-rooms, and then said farewell to the gentlemen, who went away early the next morning, but my husband stopped with me.

It is easy to guess my thoughts when at home once more, I began to undress for the night. I was brushing my hair in front of my looking-glass, and my husband, delighted with the day's outing, was very gay and tender.

I was in my shift, that clung tightly to my figure behind, and showed the seductive shape of my backside. I could see in the glass that Charles was looking at it, and that his eyes sparkled.

'Aha!' said I to myself, 'can it be possible that for once in a way he will be able to do it to me twice in the same day?'

I wanted him to make me and coquettishly struck an attitude that threw out into still greater relief what I knew was one of my greatest beauties; then negligently putting one foot on a chair, taking care that my chemise should be more raised than was absolutely necessary, I undid my garter.

This play succeeded. Charles, also in his shirt, got up, and coming nearer me kissed me on the neck, and put his hand between the cheeks of my bottom.

'Oh! oh!' said I, turning round and returning his kiss, 'whatever ails you to-night?'

'My dear wife, I find that you are extremely handsome!'

'Am I not the same every day?'

'Oh, yes; but this evening still more so!'

'Well, what are you driving at? – come!'

So saying, I put my hand on his instrument, that stood a little, although far from being in a proper state of erection.

'You see that you can't do anything!'

'Oh, yes, I can! Prithee caress him a little bit!'

'What makes you so excited?'

'Why, his . . . his . . .'

'Well now – what?'

'Your beautiful bottom!'

'Indeed, sir, Well, you shan't see any more of it!'

As supple as a kitten, I trussed up my linen with one hand, so that my posteriors were naked, while my front parts were reflect-

Cras amet qui nunquam amavit,
quique amavit cras amet.

*Let those love now, who never lov'd
before:*
*Let those who always lov'd, now love
the more.*

ORIGIN UNKNOWN

ed in the mirror; at the same time my other hand had not loosened its grasp, and cleverly excited what it held. I soon had the satisfaction to feel it get hard. Wishing to profit by his momentary desire, I made Charles sit and got striding over him, but I soon found that such a position stretched me too much, and, widening the particular part, was quite unsuited for his thin tool.

I got up, and had to begin all over again . . . I was too excited to be baulked, and once more started the caress of my agile hand. I resolved to do my best, and he helped, so that soon I was pleased to see it once more in its most splendid state! Then I drew a chair to the glass, placed one foot upon it and the other on the ground, and put it in from behind.

Charles, led on by me till he was almost beside himself, did it in such a manner that I spent three times.

———— ◊ ————

———— ◊ ————

Before following 'Hector's horse' (or at least the sexual posture known by that endearing name in the Classical world) through the darker byways of literature, it is valuable to look through the stud book. In India the sexual posture in which the woman rides the man (see page 10) has always had a special significance. Even today, traders in the bazaar will show those erotic miniatures to potential customers first because they are 'naughtier'. The reasons for this are obscure, but may have something to do with the reversal of the normal order in a society which is traditionally male-dominated. It may even be risqué because it symbolizes the hermetic Tantric concept of an all-powerful Goddess. This position is described in the *Ratikallolini*: 'She whose dark eyes are like fallen lotus petals takes your penis and guides it into her vulva, then clings tight to you and shakes her buttocks, this is Charunarikshita, Lovely Lady in Charge.'

The Chinese and Japanese call this position 'Wailing Monkey Climbing a Tree', an interesting but less homely name for it than 'Hector's horse'. Quite how the idea started that Andromache was fond of making love to the Trojan hero in this way is unknown. Martial conjures up a colourful domestic scene. 'Behind the doors the Phrygian slaves would be masturbating, every time Andromache mounted her Hector horse fashion.' Ovid disagrees on technical grounds that do not seem to make much sense. 'A little woman may get astride her horse; but tall and majestic as she was, the Theban bride never mounted the Hectorean horse.' Horace describes a prostitute who 'naked in the lamplight, plied with wanton wiles and moving buttocks the horse beneath her'. Four centuries earlier Aristophanes has Lysistrata remark, 'Women love to get on horseback and to stay there!' And in *The Wasps* the Greek playwright even makes a *double entendre*. When Xanthias asks his lover to ride him, she puns on the name of a former tyrant and the Greek for horse: 'Shall you revive the tyranny of Hippias then?'

The 'horse of Hector' was well known in the Renaissance. The lustful abbot uses it in the fourth story of Boccaccio's *Decameron*.

'Who will know? No one will ever know; and sin that is hidden is half forgiven; this chance may never come again; so, methinks, it were the part of wisdom to take the boon which God bestows.' So musing, with an altogether different purpose from that with which he had come, he drew near the girl, and softly bade her to be comforted, and besought her not to weep; and so little by little he came at last to show her what he would be at. The girl, being made neither of iron nor of adamant, was readily induced to gratify the abbot, who after bestowing upon her many an embrace and kiss, got upon the monk's bed, where, being sensible, perhaps, of the disparity between his reverend portliness and her tender youth, and fearing to injure her by his excessive weight, he refrained from lying upon her, but laid her upon him, and in that manner disported himself with her for a long time.

ABOVE One of a series of 20 nineteenth-century German erotic 'medallions' based on Renaissance and Classical visual and textual sources.

LEFT Infinite wealth and leisure in a polygamous society can lead to some strange inventions. Whether this nineteenth-century painting from Jaipur is an amusing invention of the artist or the record of an experiment is not known.

This sexual position was one of the sixteen famous sexual 'postures' which Giulio Romano originally drew on a wall in the Vatican to scandalize everyone because Pope Clement VI was late in paying him. These were turned into engravings by Marcantonio Raimondi and published together with ribald erotic sonnets by Pietro Aretino in Venice in 1527. They were greeted with a storm of protest, which continued long after his death, and the anti-clerical nature of much of Aretino's writing even caused the Inquisition to destroy copies of his work at one time. For that reason only the sonnets remain, and none of the original engravings – only copies and fragments. Aretino's *Sonetti Lussuriosi* ('Lustful Sonnets') is one of the most famous pieces of erotica in the world – and the most elusive. Casanova records that he made good use of the book in his *Memoirs*:

'No, no. Let us go to bed, or Love will challenge Apollo to a duel.'

'An excellent idea! Take this pencil and write. At the moment I am Apollo.'

She then dictated the following four lines:

Je ne me battrai pas. Je te cède la place.
Si Venus est ma sœur, commune est notre race.
Je sais faire des vers. Un moment de perdu
Ne pourra pas déplaire à l'amour convaincu.

(I will not fight. I yield the ground to you.
If Venus is my sister, we are kindred.
I can write verses. A moment lost
Cannot offend a confident Love.)

ABOVE AND BELOW Engravings from a series attributed to the French artist Jaques Philippe Caresme (1734–96).

I thereupon asked her pardon on my knees, admitting that she was also versed in mythology; but could I suppose that a Venetian lady of twenty-two who had been brought up in a convent could be so talented? She said that she had an insatiable desire to convince me that she deserved my heart, and she asked me if I thought her a shrewd gamester.

'Shrewd enough to make the banker tremble.'

'I do not always play so high, but having taken you as my partner I defied Fortune. Why did you not play?'

'Because having lost four thousand zecchini during the last week of the year, I had no money left; but I will play tomorrow and Fortune will favor me. Meanwhile here is a little book I took from your boudoir. It is Pietro Aretino's postures. In these three hours I want to try some of them.'

'That is very like you. But some of them are impossible and even silly.'

'True, but four are very interesting.'

Casanova gives the ultimate virtuoso performance of this lovemaking position, involving real as well as symbolic horses, and even a postilion! The student at this master-class is a farmer's young bride who finds herself in a two-wheeled carriage with Casanova.

'Oh my God!' said the bride. 'We are in for a storm.'

'Yes, and though the chaise is covered, the rain will ruin your dress, I'm sorry to say.'

'What do I care about my dress? It's the thunder I'm afraid of.'

'Stop up your ears.'

'And the lightning?'

'Postilion, take us somewhere where we can find shelter.'

'The nearest houses,' he answered, 'are half a league from here, and in half an hour the storm will be over.'

So saying, he drives calmly on. There is a flash of lightning, then another, thunder rumbles, and the poor woman is shaking all over. The rain comes down. I take off my cloak to use it to cover us both in front; and, heralded by an enormous flash, the lightning strikes a hundred paces ahead. The horses rear, and the poor lady is seized by spasmodic convulsions. She throws herself on me and clasps me in her arms. I bend forward to pick up the cloak, which had fallen to our feet, and, as I pick it up, I raise her skirts with it. Just as she is trying to pull them down again, there is another flash of lightning, and her terror deprives her of the power to move. Wanting to put the cloak over her again, I draw

ABOVE The Swiss artist Henry Fuseli produced many beautiful erotic drawings in London between 1790 and 1820. This is one of his courtesan scenes: remarkable for its exquisite draughtsmanship and the usual celebration of hair which held a fetishistic fascination for Fuseli.

her toward me; she literally falls on me, and I quickly put her astride me. Since her position could not be more propitious, I lose no time, I adjust myself to it in an instant by pretending to settle my watch in the belt of my breeches. Realizing that if she did not stop me at once, she could no longer defend herself, she makes an effort, but I tell her that if she does not pretend to have fainted, the postilion will turn and see everything. So saying, I leave her to call me an impious monster to her heart's content, I clasp her by the buttocks, and carry off the most complete victory that ever a skillful swordsman won. The rain coming down in torrents and the wind blowing straight in our faces, she is reduced to telling me with the greatest seriousness that I am ruining her reputation, for the postilion must be able to see her.

'I can see him,' I answered, 'and he has no idea of turning around, and even if he did my cloak covers us both completely; be reasonable and act as if you were in a faint, for I tell you I have no intention of letting you go.'

She gives in, at the same time asking me how I can defy the lightning with such impious daring; I answer that the lightning is on my side, she is inclined to believe me, she has lost almost all her fear, and having seen and felt my ecstasy, she asks me if I have finished. I laugh and answer no, I want her consent until the storm is over. 'Consent, or I will pull off my cloak.'

'You are a monster who will have made me miserable for the rest of my days. Are you satisfied now?'

'No.'

'What do you want?'

'A flood of kisses.'

'Oh, how wretched I am! Well, there you are!'

'Tell me that you forgive me. Admit that I have given you pleasure.'

'Yes. You can see that for yourself. I forgive you.'

At that I wiped her off, and when I asked her to do as much for me, I saw that she was smiling.

'Tell me that you love me,' I said.

'No, because you are an atheist and Hell awaits you.'

. . . We reached Pasiano before any of the others. She had hardly got out of the chaise before she ran and locked herself in her room while I was looking for a scudo to give to the postilion. He was laughing.

'Why are you laughing?'

'You know why.'

'Here is a ducato for you. But hold your tongue.'

ABOVE A watercolour illustration for an edition of Casanova's *Memoirs* made by the French artist Georges Pavis in 1920. BELOW A French miniature painted in the 1830s.

The Genovese merchant observed by the young Fanny Hill may have known the Classical name for his action, but he was busy enjoying himself and Fanny's education on her own admission was 'till past fourteen . . . no better than very vulgar'.

The young foreigner was sitting down, fronting us, on the couch, with Polly upon one knee, who had her arms round his neck, whilst the extreme whiteness of her skin was not undelightfully contrasted by the smooth glossy brown of her lover's.

But who could count the fierce, unnumber'd kisses given and taken? in which I could often discover their exchanging the velvet thrust, when both their mouths were double tongued, and seemed to favour the mutual insertion with the greatest gusto and delight.

In the meantime, his red-headed champion, that had so lately fled the pit, quell'd and abash'd, was now recover'd to the top of his condition, perk'd and crested up between Polly's thighs, who was not wanting, on her part, to coax and keep it in good humour, stroking it, with her head down, and received even its velvet tip between the lips of not its proper mouth: whether she did this out of any particular pleasure, or whether it was to render it more glib and easy of entrance, I could not tell; but it had such an effect, that the young gentleman seem'd by his eyes, that sparkled with more excited lustre, and his inflamed countenance, to receive increase of pleasure. He got up, and taking Polly in his arms, embraced her, and said something too softly for me to hear, leading her withal to the foot of the couch, and taking delight to slap

Would you have fresh cheese and
*   cream?*
Julia's breast can give you them:
And if more; each nipple cries,
To your cream, here's strawberries.

FRESH CHEESE AND CREAM
ROBERT HERRICK (1591–1674)

LEFT Heliogravure produced subtle tones with beautiful modelling of nude subjects: the process was never used to better effect than in the version of Aretino's sonnets published in France in 1892 from which this illustration comes.

her thighs and posterior with that stiff sinew of his, which hit them with a spring that he gave it with his hand, and made them resound again, but hurt her about as much as he meant to hurt her, for she seemed to have as frolic a taste as himself.

But guess my surprise, when I saw the lazy young rogue lie down on his back, and gently pull down Polly upon him, who giving way to his humour, straddled, and with her hands conducted her blind favourite to the right place; and following her impulse, ran directly upon the flaming point of this weapon of pleasure, which she stak'd herself upon, up pierc'd, and infix'd to the extremest hair-breadth of it: thus she sat on him a few instants, enjoying and relishing her situation, whilst he toyed with her provoking breasts. Sometimes she would stop to meet his kiss: but presently the sting of pleasure spurr'd them up to fiercer action; then began the storm of heaves, which, from the undermost combatant, were thrusts at the same time, he crossing his hands over her, and drawing her home to him with a sweet violence: the inverted strokes of anvil over hammer soon brought on the critical period, in which all the signs of a close conspiring ecstasy informed us of the *point* they were at.

BELOW This Rowlandson print appeared in the collection *Pretty Little Games for Young Ladies and Gentlemen with Pictures of good English Sports and Pastimes.*

Frank Harris was no stranger to this particular refinement of passion and seems to have acquitted himself as heroically as Hector. The first encounter he describes is with the unfortunate Mrs Mayhew who – try as she might, and she does try – never quite seems to satisfy Frank.

The next moment I began caressing her red clitoris with my hot, stiff organ: Lorna sighed deeply once or twice and her eyes turned up; slowly I pushed my prick in to the full and drew it out again to the lips, then in again, and I felt her warm love-juice gush as she drew up her knees even higher to let me further in. 'Oh, it's divine,' she sighed, 'better even than the first time,' and, when my thrusts grew quick and hard as the orgasm shook me, she writhed down on my prick as I withdrew, as if she would hold it, and as my seed spirted into her, she bit my shoulder and held her legs tight as if to keep my sex in her. We lay a few moments bathed in bliss. Then, as I began to move again to sharpen the sensation, she half rose on her arm. 'Do you know,' she said, 'I dreamed yesterday of getting on you and doing it to you, do you mind if I try?'

'No, indeed!' I cried. 'Go to it, I am your prey!' She got up smiling and straddled kneeling across me, and put my cock into her pussy and sank down on me with a deep sigh. She tried to move up and down on my organ and at once came up too high and had to use her hand to put my Tommy in again; then she sank down on it as far as possible. 'I can sink down all right,' she cried, smiling at the double meaning, 'but I cannot rise so well! What fools we women are, we can't master even the act of love; we are so awkward!'

'Your awkwardness, however, excites me,' I said.

'Does it?' she cried. 'Then I'll do my best,' and for some time she rose and sank rhythmically; but, as her excitement grew, she just let herself lie on me and wiggled her bottom till we both came.

Later Frank experiences bliss under the tutelage of a natural, the black maidservant Sophy. Her technique probably counts as 'Hector's horse'; but, clearly, it is not always possible to be too precise about the refinements of passion.

Her eyes opened brightly. 'Shu!' she cried. 'If you want to do love again, I show you!' The next moment, I was in her and now she kept even better time than at first and somehow or other the thick, firm lips of her sex seemed to excite me more than anyone had ever excited me. Instinctively the lust grew in me and I quickened and as I came to the short, hard strokes, she suddenly slipped her legs together under me and closing them tightly held my sex as in a firm grip and then began 'milking' me – no other word conveys the meaning – with extraordinary skill and speed, so that, in a moment, I was gasping and choking with the intensity of the sensation and my seed came in hot jets while she continued the milking movement, tireless, indefatigable!

ABOVE AND BELOW Drawings from the extraordinary series of erotic studies made by the German artist Johannes Martini, who was born in Chemnitz in 1866.

'What a marvel you are,' I exclaimed as soon as I got breath enough to speak, 'the best bedfellow I've ever had; wonderful, you dear, you!'

All glowing with my praise, she wound her arms about my neck and mounted me as Lorna Mayhew had done once; but what a difference! Lorna was so intent on gratifying her own lust that she often forgot my feelings altogether and her movements were awkward in the extreme; but Sophy thought only of me and, whereas Lorna was always slipping my sex out of her sheath, Sophy in some way seated herself on me and then began rocking her body back and forth while lifting it a little at each churning movement, so that my sex in the grip of her firm, thick lips had a sort of double movement. When she felt me coming as I soon did, she

OPPOSITE One of a series of 40 erotic drawings by Mihály Zichy, published in Leipzig five years after his death in 1906.
LEFT On completion of printing in 1892, private subscribers were offered a hand-coloured version of the series from which this illustration was taken. The edition was limited to 500 numbered copies.

twirled half round on my organ half a dozen times with a new movement and then began rocking herself again, so that my seed was dragged out of me, so to speak, giving me indescribably acute, almost painful sensations. I was breathless, thrilling with her every movement.

'Had you any pleasure, Sophy?' I asked as soon as we were lying side by side again.

'Shuah!' she said smiling. 'You're very strong, and you,' she asked, 'were you pleased?'

'Great God,' I cried, 'I felt as if all the hairs of my head were travelling down my backbone like an army! You are extraordinary, you dear!'

PART THREE

Forbidden fruit

'Did you miss me?
Come and kiss me.
Never mind my bruises,
Hug me, kiss me, suck my juices
Squeezed from goblin fruits for you,
Goblin pulp and goblin dew.
Eat me, drink me, love me;
Laura, make much of me:
For your sake I have braved the glen
And had to do with goblin merchant men.'

Laura started from her chair,
Flung her arms up in the air,
Clutched her hair:

'Lizzie, Lizzie, have you tasted
For my sake the fruit forbidden?
Must your light like mine be hidden,
Your young life like mine be wasted,
Undone in mine undoing
And ruined in my ruin,
Thirsty, cankered, goblin-ridden?'

FROM *GOBLIN MARKET*, CHRISTINA ROSSETTI

BELOW An etching made by the Belgian artist Martin van Maele to illustrate *Histoire Comique de Francion.*

The forbidden fruit was always sex: that was the apple which Eve gave to Adam, a symbol of her sexuality (the serpent can speak for himself – he usually does). Writers in every culture have used fruit metaphors to describe sex. Nature has aided and abetted the poets in this lascivious idea; a banana is much like a penis, the inside of the apple resembles the vulva, nipples are berries, peaches buttocks, and so on. The world's erotic literature drips with fruit juice (and wine and honey).

Eating fruit is an enjoyable oral experience and orality is of course an important part of our sexuality. The eating of fruit and oral sex are both pleasurable and sufficiently similar to work as metaphors of each other. Fellatio and cunnilingus are potentially still more pleasurable, of course, because they involve genital as well as oral stimulation (so far as we know, fruit does not enjoy being eaten).

All this explains why men and women (and poets) can enjoy fruit and oral sex; but it raises two questions. Why should fruit (pleasure) be forbidden? And why should oral sex be in this part of the anthology which is concerned with the forbidden? This is not the place to attempt to answer the first question at length. All we need to know is that the sinfulness of pleasure – sex in particular – is a Judaeo-Christian concept. Sex is wrapped around with taboos and controlled with regulations in all human societies: the innocent Pacific island of our imagination is as much a myth as the Garden of Eden (in fact, it is the same myth). What is important is how, and how much, this powerful thing is controlled. It is to be regretted that misogynistic Biblical lawmakers from Ezekiel to St Paul hit upon the idea of making sex sinful in order to control it.

This explains forbidden fruit. But since this entire anthology concerns forbidden fruit – and this section of it that which has been most forbidden – why is oral sex dealt with here? We cannot blame this on the Judaeo-Christian tradition. Listen to the Roman writer Martial, a pagan and not noted for his shyness in sexual matters: 'All night long I possessed a lewd young woman, I never knew anyone so licentious. Tired of a thousand postures, I asked for the puerile service [sodomy]; before I had done asking, she turned at once in compliance. Laughing and blushing I asked for something worse than that – the wanton consented instantly.'

BELOW *Orgy of Bacchantes* by Jaques Philippe Caresme. Appropriately enough, the artist chose watercolour as the medium.

We, nowadays, may find it strange to think of oral sex as being more unusual or wicked than sodomy, but that was certainly the view of Roman and Greek society, a view to which the works of numerous writers testify. It is too convenient to blame Old Testament prophets for everything. Why do we make such distinctions? Here is a later Jewish prophet, Sigmund Freud, having a joke about sodomy.

It is disgust which stamps that sexual aim as a perversion. I hope, however, I shall not be accused of partisanship when I assert that people who try to account for this disgust by saying that the organ in question serves the function and comes in contact with excrement . . . are not much more to the point than hysterical girls who account for their disgust of the male genital by saying that it serves to void urine.

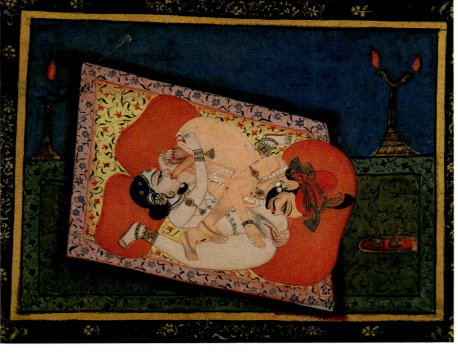

RIGHT Royal lovers enjoying the lovemaking posture known as Kakila, the Crow Position. Bundi, India, eighteenth century.

Vatsyayana in his *Kama Sutra* is quite offhand about 'congress in the anus' but says that lovemaking in water 'is improper because forbidden by religious law'. He has more surprises for those with fixed ideas on oral lovemaking.

The male servants of some men carry on the mouth congress with their masters. It is also practised by some citizens, who know each other well, among themselves. Some women of the harem, when they are amorous, do the acts of the mouth on the yonis of one another, and some men do the same thing with women. The way of doing this (i.e. of kissing the yoni) should be known from kissing the mouth. When a man and woman lie down in an inverted order, i.e. with the head of the one towards the

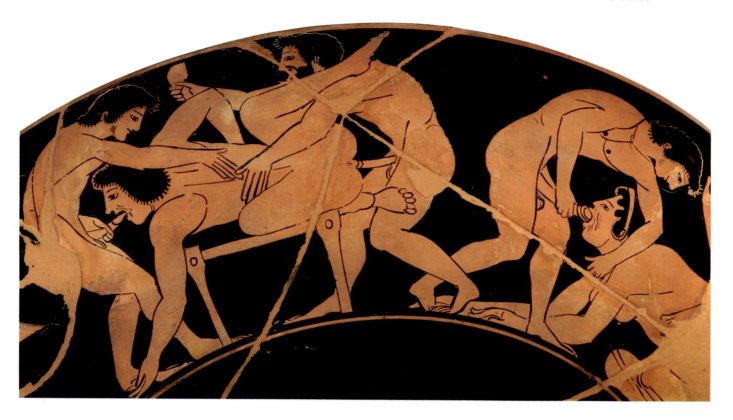

feet of the other and carry on this congress, it is called the 'congress of a crow'.

In ancient India fellatio was enjoyed by heterosexual men but was normally performed by male eunuchs and only rarely by 'unchaste and wanton women'. Vatsyayana's entire section on technique concerns male fellators.

ABOVE Greek and Roman writers regarded oral sex as very exotic sexual fare, although this does not seem to have inhibited the revellers depicted on this Attic cup attributed to the artist Skythes.

OF THE AUPARISHTAKA OR MOUTH CONGRESS

There are two kinds of eunuchs, those that are disguised as males, and those that are disguised as females. Eunuchs disguised as females imitate their dress, speech, gestures, tenderness, timidity, simplicity, softness and bashfulness. . . . These eunuchs derive their imaginable pleasure, and their livelihood from this kind of congress, and they lead the life of courtesans. . .

Eunuchs disguised as males keep their desires secret, and when they wish to do anything they lead the life of shampooers. Under the pretence of shampooing, a eunuch of this kind embraces and draws towards himself the thighs of the man whom he is shampooing, and after this he touches the joints of his thighs and his jaghana, or central portions of his body. Then, if he finds the lingam of the man erect, he presses it with his hands and chaffs him for getting into that state. If after this, and after knowing his intention, the man does not tell the eunuch to proceed, then the latter does it of his own accord and begins the congress. . . .

Suavely the wine pouring from your lower lips has called the gold swarm. It is a crimson fruit and has called the bees. The boy who has sucked that carmine fruit is drunken, and I am drunken, and the gilded bees.

FROM THE SANSCRIT MAYURA, c. 800 AD

The following eight things are then done by the eunuch one after the other:

The nominal congress
Biting the sides
Pressing outside
Pressing inside
Kissing
Rubbing
Sucking a mango fruit
Swallowing up

At the end of each of these, the eunuch expresses his wish to stop, but when one of them is finished, the man desires him to do another, and after that is done, then the one that follows it, and so on.

When, holding the man's lingam with his hand, and placing it between his lips, the eunuch moves about his mouth, it is called the 'nominal congress'.

BELOW Although research suggests that oral sex was less popular in the West at the beginning of the century than now, it was evidently part of the generous fare offered at this Czech establishment.

When, covering the end of the lingam with his fingers collected together like the bud of a plant or flower, the eunuch presses the sides of it with his lips, using his teeth also, it is called 'biting the sides'.

When, being desired to proceed, the eunuch presses the end of the lingam with his lips closed together, and kisses it as if he were drawing it out, it is called the 'outside pressing'.

When, being asked to go on, he puts the lingam further into his mouth, and presses it with his lips and then takes it out, it is called the 'inside pressing'.

When, holding the lingam in his hand, the eunuch kisses it as if he were kissing the lower lip, it is called 'kissing'.

When, after kissing it, he touches it with his tongue everywhere, and passes the tongue over the end of it, it is called 'rubbing'.

When, in the same way, he puts the half of it into his mouth, and forcibly kisses and sucks it, this is called 'sucking a mango fruit'.

And lastly, when, with the consent of the man, the eunuch puts the whole lingam into his mouth, and presses it to the very end, as if he were going to swallow it up, it is called 'swallowing up'.

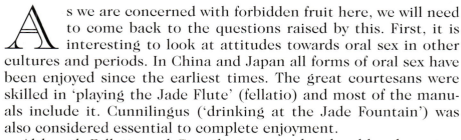

ABOVE Two of the artist Johannes Martini's sitters exploring the possibilities of 'soixante-neuf'.

As we are concerned with forbidden fruit here, we will need to come back to the questions raised by this. First, it is interesting to look at attitudes towards oral sex in other cultures and periods. In China and Japan all forms of oral sex have been enjoyed since the earliest times. The great courtesans were skilled in 'playing the Jade Flute' (fellatio) and most of the manuals include it. Cunnilingus ('drinking at the Jade Fountain') was also considered essential to complete enjoyment.

Although Fellatio and Cunnilingus sound rather like characters from the Italian *commedia dell'arte* of the seventeenth and eighteenth centuries, at that time (and indeed up to the nineteenth century) this particular forbidden fruit was not as popular as – for example – sodomy, judging by the number of pages of erotic literature devoted to it. Aretino was certainly much more interested in sodomy. Nicolas Chorier gives equal, and relatively slight, attention to both. John Cleland puts no detailed description of either in *Fanny Hill*, while devoting an entire passage to flagellation. Flagellation literature and flagellation were all the rage in the seventeenth, eighteenth and nineteenth centuries in Europe. But although some fine minds were addicted to it (Jean-Jacques Rousseau, Algernon Swinburne), we will not be examining that particular forbidden fruit, since it has the blight known as psychopathology.

No doubt it has always had its followers, but by the nineteenth century oral sex was back in fashion, though not displacing its old rival until the twentieth. We will look at fellatio first. This is the last time we will hear from Mrs Mayhew, Frank Harris's 'sad sibyl'.

'Here is something new,' she exclaimed, 'food for your vanity from my love! Mad as you make me with your love-thrusts, for at one moment I am hot and dry with desire, the next moment wet with passion, bathed in love, I could live with you all my life without having you, if you wished it, or if it would do you good. Do you believe me?'

'Yes,' I replied, continuing the love-game, but occasionally withdrawing to rub her clitoris with my sex and then slowly burying him in her cunt again to the hilt.

'We women have no souls but love,' she said faintly, her eyes dying as she spoke.

'I torture myself to think of some new pleasure for you, and yet you'll leave me, I feel you will, for some silly girl who can't feel a tithe of what I feel or give you what I give –' She began here to breathe quickly. 'I've been thinking how to give you more pleasure; let me try. Your seed, darling, is dear to me: I don't want it in my sex; I want to feel you thrill and so I want your sex in my mouth, I want to drink your essence and I will –' and suiting the action to the word, she slipped down in the bed and took my sex in her mouth and began rubbing it up and down till my seed spirted in long jets, filling her mouth while she swallowed it greedily.

'Now do I love you, Sir!' she exclaimed, drawing herself upon me again and nestling against me. 'Wait till some girl does that to you and you'll know she loves you to distraction or, better still, to self-destruction.'

'Why do you talk of any other girl?' I chided her. 'I don't imagine you going with another man; why should you torment yourself just as causelessly?'

She shook her head. 'My fears are prophetic,' she sighed. 'I'm willing to believe it hasn't happened yet, though – Ah, God, the torturing thought! The mere dread of you going with another drives me crazy; I could kill her, the bitch: why doesn't she get a man of her own? How dare she even look at you?' and she clasped me tightly to her. Nothing loath, I pushed my sex into her again and began the slow movement that excited her so quickly and me so gradually for, even while using my skill to give her the utmost pleasure, I could not help comparing and I realized surely

ABOVE The Viennese artist A1 uses his chosen medium of charcoal to capture a moment of intimacy charged with the same amalgam of melancholy and excitement as the city inhabited by both the artist and his subjects.

enough that Kate's pussy was smaller and firmer and gave me infinitely more pleasure; still I kept on for her delight. And now again she began to pant and choke and, as I continued ploughing her body and touching her womb with every slow thrust, she began to cry inarticulately with little short cries growing higher in intensity till suddenly she squealed like a shot rabbit and then shrieked with laughter, breaking down in a storm of sighs and sobs and floods of tears.

The recognition of the intimacy and special nature of oral sex is one of the threads woven into Molly Bloom's soliloquy in *Ulysses*, together with comments which suggest that more or less universally low standards of personal hygiene may have accounted for its lack of widespread popularity in the West until comparatively recent times.

. . . why arent all men like that thered be some consolation for a woman like that lovely little statue he bought I could look at him all day long curly head and his shoulders his finger up for you to listen theres real beauty and poetry for you I often felt I wanted to kiss him all over also his lovely young cock there so simple I wouldnt mind taking him in my mouth if nobody was looking as if it was asking you to suck it so clean and white he looked with his boyish face I would too in ½ a minute even if some of it went down what its only like gruel or the dew theres no danger besides hed be so clean compared with those pigs of men I suppose never dream of washing it from 1 year end to the other the most of them only thats what gives the women the moustaches Im sure itll be grand if I can only get in with a handsome young poet at my age Ill throw them the 1st thing in the morning till I see if the wishcard comes out or Ill try pairing the lady herself and see if he comes out Ill read and study all I can find or learn a bit off by heart if I knew who he likes so he wont think me stupid if he thinks all women are the same and I can teach him the other part Ill make him feel all over him till he half faints under me then hell write about me lover and mistress publicly too with our 2 photographs in all the papers when he becomes famous O but then what am I going to do about him though.

Anaïs Nin's description of fellatio, from a woman's point of view, is a clever piece of writing, matching the tension of the prose to the act described.

He was impossible to arouse except by gazing on him. And Marianne was by now in a frenzy of desire for him. The drawing was coming to an end. She knew every part of his body, the color of his skin, so golden and light, every shape of his muscles and, above all, the constantly erect sex, smooth, polished, firm, tempting.

She would approach him to arrange a piece of white cardboard

Different styles, but similar fantasies are depicted by Theo van Elsen (ABOVE) and Aubrey Beardsley (BELOW).

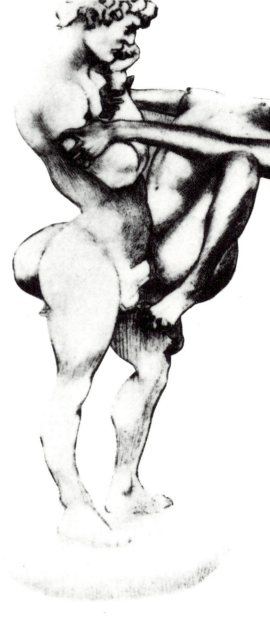

near him that would cast a whiter reflection or more shadows on his body. Then finally she lost control of herself and fell on her knees before the erect sex. She did not touch it, but merely looked and murmured, 'How beautiful it is!'

At this he was visibly affected. His whole sex became more rigid with pleasure. She kneeled very near it – it was almost within reach of her mouth – but again only said 'How beautiful it is!'

Since he did not move, she came closer, her lips parted slightly, and delicately, very delicately, she touched the tip of his sex with her tongue. He did not move away. He was still watching her face and the way her tongue flicked out caressingly to touch the tip of his sex.

She licked it gently, with the delicacy of a cat, then she inserted a small portion of it in her mouth and closed her lips around it. It was quivering. She restrained herself from doing more, for fear of encountering resistance. And when she stopped, he did not encourage her to continue. He seemed content. Marianne felt that that was all she should ask of him. She sprang to her feet and returned to her work. Inwardly she was in a turmoil. Violent images passed before her eyes. She was remembering penny movies she had seen once in Paris, of figures rolling on the grass, hands fumbling, white pants being opened by eager hands, caresses, caresses, and pleasure making the bodies curl and undulate, pleasure running over their skins like water, causing them to undulate as the wave of pleasure caught their bellies or hips, or as it ran up their spines or down their legs.

But she controlled herself with the intuitive knowledge a woman has about the tastes of the man she desires. He remained entranced, his sex erect, his body at times shivering slightly, as if pleasure coursed through it at the memory of her mouth parting to touch the smooth penis.

The day after this episode Marianne repeated her worshipful pose, her ecstasy at the beauty of his sex. Again she kneeled and prayed to this strange phallus which demanded only admiration. Again she licked it so neatly and vibrantly, sending shivers of pleasure up from the sex into his body, again she kissed it, enclosing it in her lips like some marvelous fruit, and again he trembled. Then, to her amazement, a tiny drop of a milky-white, salty substance dissolved in her mouth, the precursor of desire, and she increased her pressure and the movements of her tongue.

When she saw that he was dissolved with pleasure, she stopped, divining that perhaps if she deprived him now he might make a gesture towards fulfillment. At first he made no motion. His sex was quivering, and he was tormented with desire, then suddenly she was amazed to see his hand moving towards his sex as if he were going to satisfy himself.

Marianne grew desperate. She pushed his hand away, took his sex into her mouth again, and with her two hands she encircled his sexual parts, caressed him and absorbed him until he came.

He leaned over with gratitude, tenderness, and murmured, 'You are the first woman, the first woman, the first woman . . .'

LEFT Zichy's wonderful drawing is as much an exploration of the depressive personality as it is of impromptu fellatio.

Cunnilingus's first Western prophet, apostle (and ultimately martyr) was Frank Harris. His success as a maker of love (his own accounts were well-attested by women) may have had not a little to do with his skill in this delicate art. This is Frank's first lesson.

As we turned off towards our bedrooms on the left, I saw that her face was glowing. At her door I stopped her. 'My kiss,' I said, and as in a dream she kissed me: *l'heure du berger* had struck.

'Won't you come to me tonight?' I whispered. 'That door leads into my room.' She looked at me with that inscrutable woman's glance, and for the first time her eyes gave themselves. That night I went to bed early and moved away the sofa, which on my side barred her door. I tried the lock but found it closed on her side, worse luck!

As I lay in bed that night about eleven o'clock, I heard and saw

My hands
Open the curtains of your being
Clothe you in a further nudity
Uncover the bodies of your body
My hands
Invent another body for your body

TOUCH
OCTAVIO PAZ (1914–   )

the handle of the door move. At once I blew out the light, but the blinds were not drawn and the room was alight with moonshine. 'May I come in?' she asked.

'May you?' I was out of bed in a jiffy and had taken her adorable soft round form in my arms. 'You darling sweet,' I cried, and lifted her into my bed. She had dropped her dressing-gown, had only a nightie on, and in one moment my hands were all over her lovely body. The next moment I was with her in bed and on her, but she moved aside and away from me.

'No, let's talk,' she said.

I began kissing her, but acquiesced, 'Let's talk.'

To my amazement, she began: 'Have you read Zola's latest book, *Nana*?'

'Yes,' I replied.

'Well,' she said, 'you know what the girl did to Nana?'

'Yes,' I replied, with sinking heart.

'Well,' she went on, 'why not do that to me? I'm desperately afraid of getting a child; you would be too in my place; why not love each other without fear?' A moment's thought told me that all roads lead to Rome and so I assented and soon I slipped down between her legs. 'Tell me please how to give you most pleasure,' I said, and gently I opened the lips of her sex and put my lips on it and my tongue against her clitoris. There was nothing repulsive in it; it was another and more sensitive mouth. Hardly had I kissed it twice when she slid lower down in the bed with a sigh, whispering, 'That's it; that's heavenly!'

Thus encouraged I naturally continued: soon her little lump swelled out so that I could take it in my lips and each time I sucked it, her body moved convulsively, and soon she opened her legs further and drew them up to let me in to the uttermost. Now I varied the movement by tonguing the rest of her sex and thrusting my tongue into her as far as possible; her movements quickened and her breathing grew more and more spasmodic, and

RIGHT A drawing by Johannes
Martini.
OPPOSITE A French watercolour,
anonymous.

when I went back to the clitoris again and took it in my lips and sucked it while pushing my forefinger back and forth into her sex, her movements became wilder and she began suddenly to cry in French, 'Oh, c'est fou! Oh, c'est fou! Oh! Oh!' And suddenly she lifted me up, took my head in both her hands, and crushed my mouth with hers, as if she wanted to hurt me.

The next moment my head was between her legs again and the game went on. Little by little I felt that my finger rubbing the top of her sex while I tongued her clitoris gave her the most pleasure, and after another ten minutes of this delightful practice she cried: 'Frank, Frank, stop! Kiss me! Stop and kiss me, I can't stand any more, I am rigid with passion and want to bite or pinch you.'

Naturally I did as I was told and her body melted itself against mine while our lips met. 'You dear,' she said, 'I love you so, and oh how wonderfully you kiss.'

'You've taught me,' I said. 'I'm your pupil.'

For the rest of his life cunnilingus was an art much practised by Frank Harris, and always enthusiastically received – no doubt to the annoyance of the guests in adjoining hotel rooms.

I managed that all our rooms should be communicating and I took the middle room, as I said, to protect them. About one o'clock the first night, I entered the side-room where Grace was sleeping. I turned up the light, pulled down the bed-clothes and lifted up her chemise; she was ideally beautiful, and the little silky triangle in front deserved all my attention. Scarcely had I begun to kiss her when she awoke . . .

That night, as I was getting into bed, Mrs Sterling knocked lightly on my door. I put out the light and crept into bed and pretended to be sleeping. Again the tap, tap! I jumped out of bed.

'Who's there?' I cried, while bolting the door into Grace's room, and then went over and half-opened the door into Mrs Sterling's. She was standing with a dressing-gown about her, halfway between the door and her bed.

'Is there anything the matter?' I said.

'There are such strange noises in this hotel,' she said. 'Some one knocked at my door and I was scared and knocked at yours.'

'First-rate!' I cried, putting my arms round her and kissing her. 'You want me?' and I drew her to the bed. She shed her cloak and in a trice I had lifted up her nightie and put her on the bed. She had taken care of herself and had not let herself get too fat, but her figure was nothing like so lovely as that of Grace. Still I had to win her, so I stooped at once to conquer and began kissing her sex. In two minutes she had come three or four times with a hundred 'ohs' and 'ahs' and sobbing exclamations. 'Did your husband ever kiss you there?' I asked.

'Never, never,' she said. 'He used to have me, but he had always finished before I really began to feel: now you excite me dreadfully and give me intense pleasure besides.'

––––––––– ◇ –––––––––

Henry Miller takes a robust look at cunnilingus in a wonderfully orchestrated piece of prose from *Tropic of Cancer* that seems simple but says a good deal – about the obsessive hold that a mental picture can sometimes take, for one thing.

'After that' – here Van Norden has to smile himself – 'after that, mind you, he tells me how she sat in the chair with her legs up . . . not a stitch on . . . and he's sitting on the floor looking up at her, telling her how beautiful she looks . . . did he tell you that she looked like a Matisse? . . . Wait a minute . . . I'd like to remember exactly what he said. He had some cute little phrase there about an odalisque . . . what the hell's an odalisque anyway? He said it in French, that's why it's hard to remember the fucking thing . . . but it sounded good. It sounded just like the sort of thing he might say. And she probably thought it was original with him . . . I suppose she thinks he's a poet or something. But listen, all this is nothing . . . I make allowance for his imagination. It's what happened after that that drives me crazy. All night long I've been tossing about, playing with these images he left in my mind. I can't get it out of my head. It sounds so real to me that if it didn't happen I could strangle the bastard. A guy has no right to invent things like that. Or else he's diseased. . . .

'What I'm getting at is that moment when, he says, he got down on his knees and with those two skinny fingers of his he spread her cunt open. You remember that? He says she was sitting there with her legs dangling over the arms of the chair and suddenly, he says, he got an inspiration. This was after he had given her a couple of lays already . . . after he had made that little spiel about Matisse. He gets down on his knees – *get this!* – and with his two fingers . . . just the tips of them, mind you . . . he opens the little petals . . . *squish-squish* . . . just like that. A

ABOVE A coloured print by an unknown artist.
OPPOSITE An anonymous French etching published in 1910.

sticky little sound . . . almost inaudible. *Squish-squish!* Jesus, I've been hearing it all night long! And then he says – as if that weren't enough for me – then he tells me he buried his head in her muff. And when he did that, so help me Christ, if she didn't swing her legs around his neck and lock him there. *That finished me!* Imagine it! Imagine a fine, sensitive woman like that swinging her legs around *his neck!* . . .'

The last word on this comes from the *Story of O*. Written by the mysterious 'Pauline Réage', it first appeared in Paris in 1954.

The weather was less warm that day than it had been hitherto. René, who had spent part of the morning swimming, was napping on the couch in a cool ground-floor room. Annoyed to see that he preferred to sleep, Jacqueline had joined O in her alcove. The sea and the sun had rendered her blonder than ever: her hair, her eyebrows, her lashes, the fur between her thighs and under her arms seemed powdered with silver, and as she was wearing no make-up at all, her mouth was the same pink as the pink flesh of her open sex. In order that Sir Stephen – whose presence, O said to herself, she would surely have divined, noticed, somehow sensed, had she been in Jacqueline's place – could see every bit of her, O took care to flex Jacqueline's knees and to maintain her legs wide apart for a while and in the full light of the lamp she had turned on at the bedside. The shutters were drawn, the room was almost dark despite the slivers of light that penetrated between cracks in the wood. For nigh on to an hour Jacqueline moaned under O's caresses, and finally, her nipples erected, her arms flung over her head, clutching the wooden bars at the head of her bed, she began to scream when O, dividing the lips fringed

with pale hair, set quietly and slowly to biting the tiny inflamed morsel of flesh protruding from the cowl formed by the juncture of those sweet and delicate little labia. O felt it heat and rise under her tongue, and, nipping mercilessly, fetched cry after cry from Jacqueline until she broke like a pane of glass, and relaxed, soaked from joy. Then O sent her into her room, where she went to sleep; she was awake again and ready when at five René came to take her and Nathalie down to the water for a sail; they used to go sailing in the late afternoon, when a bit of breeze usually rose.

ABOVE A French drawing in ink over pencil dating from 1930.
BELOW A drawing by the German artist Franz von Bayros, a follower of Beardsley and one of the last prophets of Decadence.

This last extract is full of ambiguities which need to be explored. It was written by a woman to please men. The fact that it is a lesbian scene does not detract from (indeed even enhances) its appeal for men. Like the voyeuristic Sir Stephen, the heterosexual male is happy to look on. The heterosexual female response to the extract would generally be neutral, or possibly marginally positive since it is well-written and explicitly erotic. Would the heterosexual male response to a well-written male homosexual encounter be the same? And would a woman find it positively erotic as men do lesbian scenes? Here is a chance to find out. The novel *Teleny*, or *The Reverse of the Medal*, was printed as a private edition in 1893. It is the work of several hands; there is good evidence that Oscar Wilde was among them.

'I love you!' he whispered, 'I love you madly! I cannot live without you any longer.'

'Nor can I,' said I faintly; 'I have struggled against my passion in vain, and now I yield to it, not tamely, but eagerly, gladly. I am yours, Teleny! Happy to be yours, yours for ever and yours alone!'

For all answer there was a stifled hoarse cry from his innermost breast; his eyes were lighted up with a flash of fire; his craving amounted to rage; it was that of a wild beast seizing his prey; that of the lonely male finding at last a mate. Still his intense eagerness was more than that; it was also a soul issuing forth to meet another soul. It was a longing of the senses, and a mad intoxication of the brain.

Could this burning, unquenchable fire that consumed our bodies be called lust? We clung as hungrily to one another as the famished animal does when it fastens on the food it devours; and as we kissed each other with ever-increasing greed, my fingers were feeling his curly hair, or paddling the soft skin of his neck. Our legs being clasped together, his phallus, in strong erection, was rubbing against mine no less stiff and stark. We were, however, always shifting our position, so as to get every part of our bodies in as close contact as possible; and thus feeling, clasping, hugging, kissing, and biting each other, we must have looked, on that bridge amid the thickening fog, like two damned souls suffering eternal torment.

The hand of Time had stopped; and I think we should have continued goading each other in our mad desire until we had

quite lost our senses – for we were both on the verge of madness – had we not been stopped by a trifling incident.

A belated cab – wearied by the day's toil – was slowly trudging its way homeward. The driver was sleeping on his box; the poor, broken-down jade, with its head drooping almost between its knees, was likewise slumbering – dreaming, perhaps, of unbroken rest, of new-mown hay, of the fresh and flowery pastures of its youth; even the slow rumbling of the wheels had a sleepy, purring, snoring sound in its irksome sameness.

'Come home with me,' said Teleny, in a low, nervous and trembling voice; 'come and sleep with me,' added he, in the soft, hushed and pleading tone of the lover who would fain be understood without words.

I pressed his hands for all answer.

'Will you come?'

'Yes,' I whispered, almost inaudibly.

This low, hardly-articulate sound was the hot breath of vehement desire; this lisped monosyllable was the willing consent to his eagerest wish.

Then he hailed the passing cab, but it was some moments before the driver could be awakened and made to understand what was wanted of him.

As I stepped in the vehicle, my first thought was that in a few minutes Teleny would belong to me. This thought acted upon my nerves as an electric current, making me shiver from head to foot.

My lips had to articulate the words 'Teleny will be mine,' for me to believe it. He seemed to hear the noiseless murmur of my lips, for he clasped my head between his hands, and kissed me again and again.

Then, as if feeling a pang of remorse – 'You do not repent, do you?' he asked.

'How can I?'

'And you will be mine – mine alone?'

'I never was any other man's, nor ever shall be.'

'You will love me for ever?'

'And ever.'

'This will be our oath and our act of possession,' added he.

Thereupon he put his arms around me and clasped me to his breast. I entwined my arms round him. By the glimmering, dim light of the cab-lamps I saw his eyes kindle with the fire of madness. His lips – parched with the thirst of long-suppressed desire, of the pent-up craving of possession – pouted towards mine with a painful expression of dull suffering. We were again sucking up each other's being in a kiss – a kiss more intense, if possible, than the former one. What a kiss that was!

The flesh, the blood, the brain, and that undefined subtler part of our being seemed all to melt together in an ineffable embrace.

A kiss is something more than the first sensual contact of two bodies; it is the breathing forth of two enamoured souls.

But a criminal kiss long withstood and fought against, and therefore long yearned after, is beyond this; it is as luscious as forbidden fruit; it is a glowing coal set upon the lips; a fiery

Today in the afternoon love passed
Over his perfect flesh, and on his lips.
Over his flesh, which is the mould
Of beauty, passed love's fever,
  uncontrolled
By any ridiculous shame for the form
  of the enjoyment . . .

FROM *HE CAME TO READ*
C. P. CAVAFY (1863–1933)

brand that burns deep, and changes the blood into molten lead or scalding quicksilver.

Teleny's kiss was really galvanic, for I could taste its sapidity upon my palate. Was an oath needed, when we had given ourselves to one another with such a kiss? An oath is a lip-promise which can be, and is, often forgotten. Such a kiss follows you to the grave.

Whilst our lips clung together, his hand slowly, imperceptibly, unbuttoned my trousers, and stealthily slipped within the aperture, turning every obstacle in its way instinctively aside, then it lay hold of my hard, stiff, and aching phallus which was glowing like a burning coal.

This grasp was as soft as a child's, as expert as a whore's, as strong as a fencer's. . . .

Some people, as we all know, are more magnetic than others. Moreover, while some attract, others repel us. Teleny had – for me, at least – a supple, mesmeric, pleasure-giving fluid in his fingers. Nay, the simple contact of his skin thrilled me with delight.

My own hand hesitatingly followed the lead his hand had given, and I must confess the pleasure I felt in paddling him was really delightful.

Our fingers hardly moved the skin of the penis; but our nerves were so strained, our excitement had reached such a pitch, and the seminal ducts were so full, that we felt them overflowing. There was, for a moment, an intense pain, somewhere about the root of the penis – or rather, within the very core and centre of the reins, after which the sap of life began to move slowly, slowly, from within the seminal glands; it mounted up the bulb of the urethra, and up the narrow column, somewhat like mercury within the tube of a thermometer – or rather, like the scalding and scathing lava within the crater of a volcano.

It finally reached the apex; then the slit gaped, the tiny lips parted, and the pearly, creamy fluid oozed out – not all at once in a gushing jet, but at intervals, and in huge, burning tears.

OPPOSITE Study of a nude boy by a contemporary artist.
ABOVE AND BELOW Drawings from Aubrey Beardsley's *Lysistrata* which had to be published underground following the Oscar Wilde scandal of 1895. The Decadents rushed to death before the century from which they were forever alienated: Beardsley in March and Rops in August 1898.

Roman and Greek writers (like the Arab erotologists) wrote extensively about homosexuality. There were those for whom it was a lifetime's passion, of course, like the general (and later emperor) Galba of whom Suetonius wrote: 'He was much given to the intercourse between men . . . it is said that when Icelus, one of his old bedfellows, came to Spain to tell him of Nero's death, he kissed him closely before everyone present and asked him at once to be depilated . . . !'

For other males in Classical times, homosexuality was a passing phase in their life. The Greeks have indeed given us a name for this relationship: Socratic love. In return for education and board and lodging, a youth would grant his tutor/protector sexual favours, but on reaching a certain age they would part, often with tears, the young man to marry, his mentor to face loneliness or perhaps to find another companion.

Bisexuality and homosexuality were common among the Roman patrician class in the first century AD and a favourite target for Martial and Juvenal. Many of Martial's epigrams were savage; this is among the milder ones: 'Pluck out the hair from breast and legs and arms; keep your member cropped and ringed with short hair; all this, we know, you do for your mistress' sake, Labienus. But for whom do you depilate your posteriors?' His attacks on the lesbian secret societies of Rome were no less harsh.

Our society has moved on since it destroyed Oscar Wilde – it needed to. Now the tragedy of AIDS has rekindled the flames of prejudice. Our greatest playwright, Shakespeare, had a homosexual love affair and wrote about it in the *Sonnets*. He also wrote *Twelfth Night*, in which a boy actor plays a girl, who dresses as a boy, who falls in love with a man, who . . . a comedy with a message which they tend to leave out of the notes in school editions: that gender is less important than we might suppose. To end this topic, here is a heady cocktail of orality, anality and ambiguity from Anaïs Nin.

BELOW A hand-coloured etching by the German artist Carl Breuer-Courth dated 1920.

Under their feet was a big white fur. They fell on this, the three bodies in accord, moving against each other to feel breast against breast and belly against belly. They ceased to be three bodies. They became all mouths and fingers and tongues and senses. Their mouths sought another mouth, a nipple, a clitoris. They lay entangled, moving very slowly. They kissed until the kissing became a torture and the body grew restless. Their hands always found yielding flesh, an opening. The fur they lay on gave off an animal odor, which mingled with the odors of sex.

Elena sought the fuller body of Bijou. Leila was more aggressive. She had Bijou lying on her side, with one leg thrown over Leila's shoulder, and she was kissing Bijou between the legs. Now and then Bijou jerked backwards, away from the stinging kisses and bites, the tongue that was as hard as a man's sex.

When she moved thus, her buttocks were thrown fully against Elena's face. With her hands Elena had been enjoying the shape of them, and now she inserted her finger into the tight little aperture. There she could feel every contraction caused by Leila's kisses, as if she were touching the wall against which Leila moved her tongue. Bijou, withdrawing from the tongue that searched her, moved into a finger which gave her joy. Her pleasure was expressed in melodious ripples of her voice, and now and then, like a savage being taunted, she bared her teeth and tried to bite the one who was tantalizing her.

When she was about to come and could no longer defend herself against her pleasure, Leila stopped kissing her, leaving Bijou halfway on the peak of an excruciating sensation, half-crazed. Elena had stopped at the same moment.

Uncontrollable now, like some magnificent maniac, Bijou threw herself over Elena's body, parted her legs, placed herself between them, glued her sex to Elena's, and moved, moved with desperation. Like a man now, she thumped against Elena, to feel the two sexes meeting, soldering. Then as she felt her pleasure coming she stopped herself, to prolong it, fell backwards and opened her mouth to Leila's breast, to burning nipples that were seeking to be caressed.

Elena was now also in the frenzy before orgasm. She felt a hand under her, a hand she could rub against. She wanted to throw herself on this hand until it made her come, but she also wanted to prolong her pleasure. And she ceased moving. The hand pursued her. She stood up, and the hand again traveled towards her sex. Then she felt Bijou standing against her back, panting. She felt the pointed breasts, the brushing of Bijou's sexual hair against her buttocks. Bijou rubbed against her, and then slid up and down, slowly, knowing the friction would force Elena to turn so as to feel this on her breasts, sex and belly. Hands, hands everywhere at once. Leila's pointed nails buried in the softest part of Elena's shoulder, between her breast and underarm, hurting, a delicious pain, the tigress taking hold of her, mangling her. Elena's body so burning hot that she feared one more touch

ABOVE A French lithograph of 1925.

If the unexpurgated version of the *Diary* is ever published, this feminine point of view will be established more clearly. It will show that women (and I, in the *Diary*) have never separated sex from feeling, from love of the whole man.

ANAÏS NIN (1903–77)

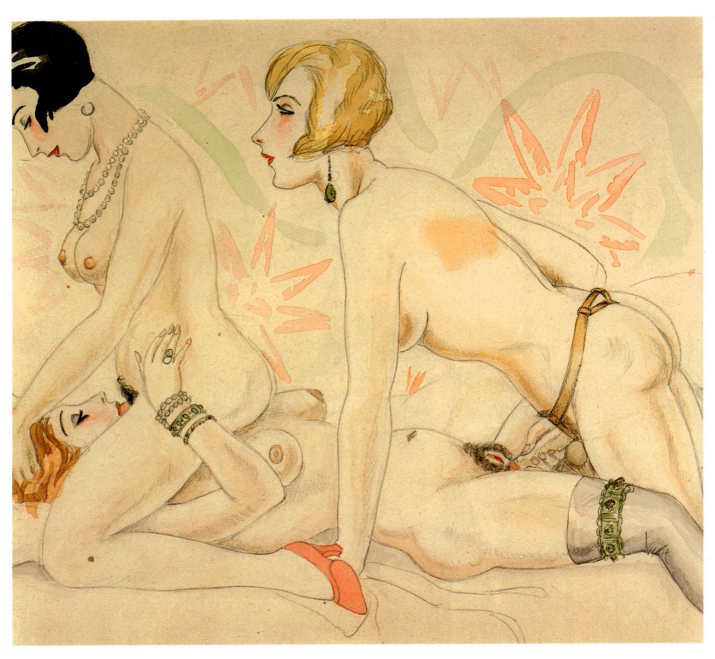

ABOVE AND OPPOSITE French
watercolours by an unknown artist
working in Paris in 1925.

would set off the explosion. Leila sensed this, and they separated.

All three of them fell on the couch. They ceased touching and looked at each other, admiring their disorder, and seeing the moisture glistening along their beautiful legs.

But they could not keep their hands away from each other, and now Elena and Leila together attacked Bijou, intent on drawing from her the ultimate sensation. Bijou was surrounded, enveloped, covered, licked, kissed, bitten, rolled again on the fur rug, tormented with a million hands and tongues. She was begging now to be satisfied, spread her legs, sought to satisfy herself by friction against the others' bodies. They would not let her.

With tongues and fingers they pryed into her, back and front, sometimes stopping to touch each other's tongue – Elena and Leila, mouth to mouth, tongues curled together, over Bijou's spread legs. Bijou raised herself to receive a kiss that would end her suspense. Elena and Leila, forgetting her, concentrated all their feelings in their tongues, flicking at each other. Bijou, impatient, madly aroused, began to stroke herself, then Leila and Elena pushed her hand away and fell upon her. Bijou's orgasm came like an exquisite torment. At each spasm she moved as if she were being stabbed. She almost cried to have it end.

Over her prone body, Elena and Leila took up their tongue-kissing again, hands drunkenly searching each other, penetrating everywhere, until Elena cried out. Leila's fingers had found her rhythm, and Elena clung to her, waiting for the pleasure to burst, while her own hands sought to give Leila the same pleasure. They tried to come in unison, but Elena came first, falling in a heap, detached from Leila's hand, struck down by the violence of her orgasm. Leila fell beside her, offering her sex to Elena's mouth. As Elena's pleasure grew fainter, rolling away, dying off, she gave Leila her tongue, flicking in the sex's mouth until Leila contracted and moaned. She bit into Leila's tender flesh. In the paroxysm of her pleasure, Leila did not feel the teeth buried there.

Elena now understood why some Spanish husbands refused to initiate their wives to all the possibilities of lovemaking – to avoid the risk of awakening in them an insatiable passion.

There are, of course, many different varieties of forbidden fruit. These are the erotic caprices which lovers sometimes have. In *Satyra Sotadica*, for example, the heroine Octavia confides to her friend that her lover Caviceo has recently been seized by an erotic whim.

You know there is in our house a gallery giving onto the garden, which is full of flowers. There Caviceo and I were promenading: he embraced me, kissed me, nibbled my lips and then thrust his hand in my bosom. 'I have a whim,' he said, 'bare your breasts, my darling!' What was I to do? His hot eyes rested on my bare bosom. 'I see Venus sleeping between your breasts,' he said, 'May I awaken her?' He then reveals himself, fiercely erect, and slides his hot, burning member between my breasts. How could I escape his blind passion? I had no choice but to bear it. His hands softly pressed my breasts together, so as to narrow the space, in which his manhood had to travel towards a new experience. Why make a long story? Stupefied as I was at this vain ridiculous imitation of Love, he inundated me with a burning libation: he had his will.

Erotic caprices may not always involve another, as in this decadent piece of self-adulation, a masturbatory fantasy involving a mirror from the pen of Anaïs Nin, which ends suitably enough with a forbidden fruit metaphor.

Thinking of Martinez, Mathilde would feel passionate. And she could not wait for his return. She looked down at her legs. From living so much indoors they had become white, very alluring, like the chalk-white complexion of the Chinese women, the morbid hothouse paleness that men, and particularly the dark-skinned Peruvians, loved. She looked at her belly, without fault, without a single line that should not be there. The pubic hair shone red-gold now in the sun.

'How do I look to him?' she asked herself. She got up and brought a long mirror towards the window. She stood it on the floor against a chair. Then she sat down in front of it on the rug and, facing it, slowly opened her legs. The sight was enchanting.

RIGHT An etching of an unconventional barre exercise by the French artist Marcel Vértes (1895–1961).

The skin was flawless, the vulva, roseate and full. She thought it was like the gum plant leaf with its secret milk that the pressure of the finger could bring out, the odorous moisture that came like the moisture of the sea shells. So was Venus born of the sea with this little kernel of salty honey in her, which only caresses could bring out of the hidden recesses of her body.

Mathilde wondered if she could bring it out of its mysterious core. With her fingers she opened the two little lips of the vulva, and she began stroking it with catlike softness. Back and forth she stroked it as Martinez did with his more nervous dark fingers. She remembered his dark fingers on her skin, such a contrast to her skin, and the thickness of them seeming to promise to hurt the skin rather than arouse pleasure by their touch. How delicately he touched it, she thought, how he held the vulva between his fingers, as if he were touching velvet. She held it now as he did, in her forefinger and thumb. With the other free hand she continued the caresses. She felt the same dissolving feeling that she felt under Martinez's fingers. From somewhere a salty liquid was coming, covering the wings of her sex; between these it now shone.

Then Mathilde wanted to know how she looked when Martinez told her to turn over. She lay on her left side and exposed her ass to the mirror. She could see her sex now from another side. She moved as she moved for Martinez. She saw her own hand appear over the little hill formed by the ass, which she began to stroke. Her other hand went between her legs and showed in the mirror from behind. This hand stroked her sex back and forth. Then a forefinger was inserted and she began to rub against it. Now she was taken with the desire to be taken from both sides, and she inserted her other forefinger into the ass hole. Now when she moved forwards she felt her finger in the front, and when she lurched back she felt the other finger, as she sometimes felt Martinez and a friend when they both caressed her at once. The approach of the orgasm excited her, she went into convulsive gestures, as if to pull away the ultimate fruit from a branch, pulling, pulling at the branch to bring down everything into a wild orgasm, which came while she watched herself in the mirror, seeing the hands move, the honey shining, the whole sex and ass shining wet between the legs.

ABOVE Two of the young debauchees Franz von Bayros was fond of depicting gaze through a glass darkly.
BELOW An unattributed sepia etching from a series apparently intended to illustrate Casanova's *Memoirs*, possibly by the French artist Georges Pavis.

Casanova devoted a lifetime to the pursuit of forbidden fruit of one kind or another. He was fond of seducing nuns, for example, and of making love to women in pairs whenever possible. This extract from the *Memoirs* concerns two sisters and may explain the voyeurism which runs through all erotica – which is indeed the essence of erotica. Like Angelica, we are imitative beings, our imaginations and appetites stirred by what we see and hear.

I put my eye to the keyhole and five minutes later saw them come in, accompanied by Don Francesco, who lit a night lamp for them and then left. After locking the door they sat down on the couch,

where I watched them undress. Lucrezia, knowing that I could hear her, told her sister to take the side of the bed toward the window. Upon which the virgin, unaware that she was observed, takes off even her shift and in this striking array crosses to the other side of the room. Lucrezia extinguishes the night light, blows out the candles, and lies down too.

Happy moments for which I hope no longer, but whose precious memory death alone can take from me! I believe I never undressed more quickly. I opened the door and fell into the arms of my Lucrezia, who said to her sister: 'It is my angel, hold your tongue and go to sleep.'

She could say no more, for our clinging mouths were no longer either organs of speech or channels for respiration. Become a single being at the same instant, we did not have the strength to restrain our first desire for more than a minute; it ran its course without the sound of a single kiss or the least movement on our part. The raging fire which urged us on was scorching us; it would have burned us had we tried to restrain it.

After a short respite, ourselves the ingenious ministers of our love and jealous of the fire which it was to rekindle in our veins, we went silently, seriously, and calmly to work drying from our fields the too copious flood which had followed the first eruption. We performed this sacred service for each other with fine linen, devoutly and in the most religious silence. After this expiation we paid homage with our kisses to all the places which we had lately flooded.

It was now my part to invite my fair enemy to begin a battle whose tactics could be known only to love, a combat which, enchanting all our senses, could have no fault but that of ending too soon; but I excelled in the art of prolonging it. When it was over, Morpheus took possession of our senses and held us in a sweet death until the moment when the light of dawn showed us in each other's scarcely opened eyes an inexhaustible spring of new desires. We surrendered to them, but it was to destroy them. A delightful destruction, which we could only accomplish by satisfying them!

'Beware of your sister,' I said; 'she might turn and see us.'

'No, my sister is charming; she loves me and she pities me. Is not that so, dear Angelica? Turn and embrace your sister, who is possessed by Venus. Turn and see what awaits you when love makes you his slave.'

Angelica, a girl of seventeen, who must have passed a hellish night, asks nothing better than an excuse to turn and show her sister that she had forgiven her. Kissing her a hundred times, she confessed that she had not slept at all.

'Forgive,' Lucrezia said, 'him who loves me and whom I adore; come, look at him, and look at me. We are as we were seven hours ago. The power of Love!'

'Hated by Angelica,' I said, 'I dare not –'

'No,' said Angelica, 'I do not hate you.'

Telling me to kiss her, Lucrezia gets on the other side of me and enjoys the spectacle of her sister in my arms, languishing and showing no signs of resistance. But feeling, even more than

love, prevents me from defrauding Lucrezia of the token of gratitude which I owed her. I clasp her frenziedly, at the same time reveling in the ecstasy I saw on the face of Angelica, who was witnessing so splendid a combat for the first time. The swooning Lucrezia implores me to stop, but finding me inexorable throws me on her sister who, far from repulsing me, clasps me to her bosom so strongly that she achieves happiness almost without my participation. *It was thus that when the Gods dwelt on earth the*

voluptuous Anaideia, in love with the soft, delightful breath of the West Wind, one day opened her arms to it and became fruitful. It was the divine Zephyrus. The fire of nature made Angelica insensible to pain; she felt only the joy of satisfying her ardent desire.

Astonished, blissfully content, and kissing us in turn, Lucrezia was as delighted to see her swoon as she was charmed to see that I continued. She wiped away the drops of sweat which dripped from my brow. Angelica finally perished for the third time, so lovingly that she ravished my soul.

Stolen apples are often sweeter, but best eaten quickly. In a real-life episode from the Victorian period, recorded in an extraordinary letter, we have much more than an amusing re-telling of a disastrous excursion. The writer who reveals himself is Edward Sellon: writer of erotica (possibly some of the anonymous pieces in this anthology), anthropologist and confirmed libertine. A month after writing this, in 1866, aged forty-eight, he shot himself in a Piccadilly hotel, leaving a cheerful erotic poem for his current lady-love and the motto *Vivat Lingam, Non Resurgam* ('Long live the phallus – I shall not rise again'). The letter was sent to H. S. Ashbee, the man believed by Gershon Legman, the authority on erotic literature, to be 'Walter'. Ashbee was the greatest collector of erotic literature of his day. His library forms the basis for the 'private case' in the British Library, where original copies of many of the Victorian and earlier works quoted in this anthology can be seen.

Because one figure was undressed
This little drawing was suppressed
It was unkind –
But never mind
Perhaps it all was for the best.

INSCRIPTION ON THE PROOF OF A DRAWING
SENT TO FRANK HARRIS
AUBREY BEARDSLEY (1872–98)

You will be very much surprised no doubt to find that I am again in England. But there are so many romances in real life that you will perhaps not be so much astonished at what I am going to relate after all.

You must know then that in our trip to the continent, (Egypt it appears was a hoax of which I was to be the victim) we were to be accompanied by a lady! I did not name this to you at the time, because I was the confidant of my friend.

On Monday evening I sat for a mortal hour in his brougham near the Wandsworth Road Railway Station waiting for the 'fair but frail,' who had done me the honor to send me a beautiful little pink note charmingly scented with violets, in which the dear creature begged me to be punctual – and most punctual I was I assure you, but alas! She kept me waiting a whole hour, during which I smoked no end of cigars.

At length she appeared, imagine my surprise! I! who had expected some swell mot or other, soon found myself seated beside the most beautiful young lady I ever beheld, so young that I could not help exclaiming, 'Why my dear you are a mere baby! how old may I be permitted to ask?' She gave me a box on the ear, exclaiming, 'Baby indeed! do you know sir, I am fifteen!!' 'And you love Mr Scarsdale very much I suppose?' said I as a feeler. 'Oh! comme ça!' she rejoined. 'Is he going to marry you at Vienna, or Egypt?' I asked. 'Who's talking of Egypt?' said she. 'Why I am I hope my dear, our dear friend invited me to accompany him up to the third Cataract, and this part of the affair, you I mean my dear, never transpired till half-an-hour before I got that pretty little note of yours.' 'Stuff!' she said, 'he was laughing at you, we go no farther than Vienna!' 'Good!' said I, 'all's fair in love and war,' and I gave her a kiss! She made no resistance, so I thrust my hand up her clothes without more ado. 'Who are you my dear?' I enquired. 'The daughter of a merchant in the city who lives at Clapham,' said she. 'Does your mother know you're out?' I ejaculated. 'I am coming out next summer,' said she. 'That is to say you were coming out next summer,' said I. 'Well I shall be married then you know,' said the innocent. 'Stuff!' said I in my turn. 'How stuff?' she asked angrily, 'do you know he has seduced me?' 'No my angel, I did not know it, but I thought as much – but don't be deceived, a man of Mr Scarsdale's birth won't marry a little cit like you.' She burst into tears. I was silent. 'Have you known him long?' she asked. 'Some years,' said I. 'And you really think he won't marry me?' 'Sure of it, my dear

BELOW A plate from Aubrey Beardsley's *Lysistrata*.

We are all in the gutter, but some of us are looking at the stars.

FROM *LADY WINDERMERE'S FAN*
OSCAR WILDE (1854–1900)

---○---

BELOW An illustration for Rochester's poems by the German artist Julius Klinger, 1909.
OPPOSITE An anonymous German watercolour dated 1917.

---○---

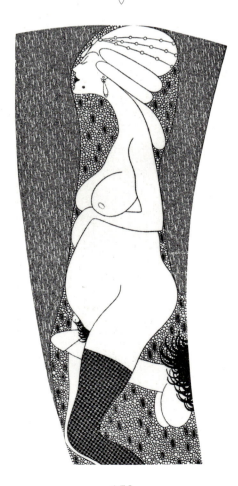

child.' 'Very well, I'll be revenged, look here, I like you!' 'Do you though! by Jove!' 'Yes, and, –' I give you my word I was into her in a moment! What bliss it was! None who have not entered the seventh heaven can fathom it! But alas! we drew near the station, and I only got one poke complete. She pressed my hand as I helped her out of the Brougham at the Chatham and Dover Station, as much as to say 'you shall have me again.' Scarsdale was there to receive her. Not to be tedious, off we started by the Mail, and duly reached Dover, went on board the boat, reached Calais, off again by train. Damned a chance did I get till we were within ten or twelve versts of Vienna. Then my dear friend fell asleep, God bless him! The two devils of passengers who had travelled with us all the way from Calais had alighted at the last station – here was a chance!! We lost not an instant. She sat in my lap, her stern towards me! God! what a fuck it was, 'See Rome and die!' said I in a rapture. This over we were having what I call a straddle fuck, when lo! Scarsdale woke up! I made a desperate effort to throw her on the opposite seat, but it was no go, he had seen us. A row of course ensued, and we pitched into one another with hearty good will. He called me a rascal for tampering with his fiancée, I called him a scoundrel for seducing so young a girl! and we arrived at Vienna! 'Damn it,' said I as I got out of the train with my lip cut and nose bleeding, 'here's a cursed piece of business.' As for Scarsdale who had received from me a pretty black eye, he drove off with the sulky fair to a hotel in the Leopoldstadt, while I found a more humble one in the Graben near St. Stephen's Cathedral, determined, as I had £15 in my pocket to stay a few days and see all I could. But as you will find in Murray a better account of what I did see than I can give you, I will not trouble you with it. I got a nice little note the next day from the fair Julia appointing a meeting the next day at the Volksgarten. How she eluded the vigilance of her gallant I don't know, but there she was sure enough in a cab – and devilish nice cabs they are in this city of Vienna, I can tell you. So we had a farewell poke and arranged for a rendezvous in England, and the next day I started and here I am, having spent all my money!

So there's the finish of my tour up the Nile to the third Cataract, to Nubia, Abu Sinnel, etcetera. It is very wrong I know, I deplore it! but you also know that what's bred in the bone, &c., so adieu, and believe me

Yours very truly
E. SELLON.

---○---

Edward Sellon translated parts of Boccaccio's *Decameron* into English, but this tale of an inventive adulterer is from J. M. Rigg's version. Her husband returning unexpectedly, Peronella pretends to be selling a barrel to Giannello, her lover.

'Here am I: what wouldst thou of me?' Quoth Giannello: – 'And who art thou? I would speak with the lady with whom I struck the bargain for this tun.' Then said the good man: – 'Have no fear,

RIGHT A latter-day Pyramus and
Thisbe drawn by Paul Gavarni
(1804–1866).

you can deal with me; for I am her husband.' Quoth then Giannello: – 'The tun seems to me sound enough; but I think you must have let the lees remain in it; for 'tis all encrusted with I know not what that is so dry, that I cannot raise it with the nail; wherefore I am not minded to take it unless I first see it scoured.' Whereupon Peronella: – 'To be sure: that shall not hinder the bargain; my husband will scour it clean.' And: – 'Well and good,' said the husband.

So he laid down his tools, stripped himself to his vest, sent for a light and a rasp, and was in the tun, and scraping away, in a trice. Whereupon Peronella, as if she were curious to see what he did, thrust her head into the vent of the tun, which was of no great size, and therewithal one of her arms up to the shoulder, and fell a saying: – 'Scrape here, and here, and there too, and look, there is a bit left here.' So, she being in this posture, directing and admonishing her husband, Giannello, who had not, that morning, fully satisfied his desire, when the husband arrived, now seeing that as he would, he might not, brought his mind to his circumstances, and resolved to take his pleasure as he might: wherefore he made up to the lady, who completely blocked the vent of the tun; and even on such wise as on the open champaign the wild and lusty horses do amorously assail the mares of Parthia, he sated his youthful appetite; and so it was that almost at the same moment that he did so, and was off, the tun was scoured, the husband came forth of it, and Peronella withdrew her head from the vent, and turning to Giannello, said: – 'Take this light, good man, and see if 'tis scoured to thy mind.' Whereupon Giannello, looking into the tun, said that 'twas in good trim, and that he was well content, and paid the husband the seven gigliats, and caused him carry the tun to his house.

The old rogue Sheikh Nefzawi has the final word on forbidden fruit in this cautionary tale from his *Perfumed Garden*. The ingenious, if uncomfortable scheme demonstrates that lust – if not love – will always find a way . . .

There was once a man who had a wife whose beauty was like that of the moon at its full. He was very jealous, for he knew all the tricks that people play. That being so, he never went out without locking the doors of the house and terrasses. One day his wife said to him:

'Why do you do that?'

'Because I know your tricks and habits.'

'What you are doing is no good; when a woman wants a thing, all precautions are useless.'

'Perhaps so! but for all that I'll fasten the doors.'

'Locking a door is no good if a woman has made up her mind to get what you are thinking of.'

'Well! if you can do anything, do it!'

As soon as her husband had gone out, the woman went to the top of the house and made a hole in the wall so that she could

Down, wanton, down! Have you no shame
That at the whisper of Love's name,
Or Beauty's, presto! up you raise
Your angry head and stand at gaze?

Poor bombard-captain, sworn to reach
The ravelin and effect a breach –
Indifferent what you storm or why,
So be that in the breach you die!

Love may be blind, but Love at least
knows what is man and what mere beast;
Or Beauty wayward, but requires
More delicacy from her squires

Tell me, my witless, whose one boast
Could be your staunchness at the post,
When were you made a man of parts
To think fine and profess the arts?

Will many-gifted Beauty come
Bowing to your bald rule of thumb,
Or Love swear loyalty to your crown?
Be gone, have done! Down, wanton, down!

Down, Wanton, Down!
Robert Graves (1895–1985)

see who was passing. At that moment a young man was going along the street; he raised his eyes, saw the woman, and desired to possess her. He asked how he could get to her. She told him he could not enter as all the doors were fastened.

'But how can we meet?' he asked.

'I will make a hole in the house door; you, when you see my husband returning from evening prayer, will wait until he has got inside the house, and then push your member through the hole in the door, opposite which I will put my vulva. In that way we can copulate – any other way will be impossible.'

So the young man watched for the husband's return and, as soon as he had seen him enter the house and close the door behind him, he went to the hole which had been cut in the door and put his member through it. The woman was also on the look-out; hardly had her husband entered, and while he was still in the courtyard, she went to the door under the pretext of seeing if it were fastened; then, hastening to put her vulva opposite the member which was sticking through the hole, she introduced it entirely into her vagina.

That done, she put out her lamp and called to her husband to bring her a light.

'Why?' he asked.

'I have dropped the jewel I wear on my breast and cannot find it.'

So the husband brought a lamp. The young man's member was still in the woman's vulva and it had just ejaculated.

'Where did your jewel fall?' asked the husband.

'There it is!' she cried; and she drew back quickly, leaving uncovered her lover's member, which was withdrawn from the vulva all wet with sperm.

At sight of this the husband fell on the ground in a violent rage and, when he got up, his wife asked:

'Well, what about your precautions?'

'May God make me repent!' was his reply.

The final word in this anthology of erotic art and literature comes from D. H. Lawrence.

And when, throughout all the wild orgasms of love
slowly a gem forms, in the ancient, once-more-molten rocks
of two human hearts, two ancient rocks, a man's heart and a
    woman's,
that is the crystal of peace, the slow hard jewel of trust,
the sapphire of fidelity.
The gem of mutual peace emerging from the wild chaos of love.

OPPOSITE Stone relief, India, eleventh century AD.

The Authors

Wystan Hugh Auden (1907–73) English (later naturalized American) poet.

William Blake (1757–1827) English poet and artist who illustrated his own poetry.

Giovanni Boccaccio (1313–75) Italian writer, born in Florence; he wrote the *Decameron* in 1348–53.

Giovanni Giacomo Casanova, Chevalier de Seingalt (1725–98) Italian adventurer, gambler, spy, writer and librarian.

C. P. Cavafy (1863–1933) Greek poet who lived mainly in Alexandria.

Nicolas Chorier (late seventeenth–early eighteenth century) French lawyer and writer.

John Cleland (1709–89) English novelist; he wrote *Fanny Hill* in 1748–9.

e. e. cummings (1894–1962) American poet whose work experimented with typographical effects.

Ernest Dowson (1867–1900) English poet, friend of Yeats.

Sigmund Freud (1856–1939) Austrian psychiatrist and psychoanalyst; he died in London.

Robert Graves (1895–1985) English poet and novelist, author of *The White Goddess*; he lived in Majorca for nearly 50 years.

Frank Harris (1856–1931) Writer and newspaper editor; born in Ireland, he lived in London and America.

Robert Herrick (1591–1674) English poet.

James Joyce (1882–1941) Irish novelist; he wrote *Ulysses* in 1922.

David Herbert Lawrence (1885–1930) British novelist, born in Nottinghamshire; he wrote *Lady Chatterley's Lover* in 1928.

Henry Miller (1891–1980) American novelist, author of *Tropic of Cancer* (1934) and *Tropic of Capricorn* (1939).

Pablo Neruda (1904–73) Chilean poet and diplomat who won the Nobel Prize in 1971.

Anaïs Nin (1903–77) French writer, brought up in New York; the publication of her seven-volume *Diary* was begun in 1931.

Octavio Paz (1914–) Mexican poet and diplomat.

Pierre de Ronsard (1524–85) French poet whose court career was interrupted by deafness.

Christina Rossetti (1830–74) English poet of Italian ancestry, sister of Dante Gabriel.

Robin Skelton (1925–) Canadian poet.

Algernon Charles Swinburne (1837–1909) English Decadent poet.

Paul Verlaine (1844–96) French poet, leading light of the Symbolists.

Oscar Wilde (1854–1900) English dramatist of Irish ancestry, born in Dublin; after imprisonment for homosexuality he was exiled to France.

John Wilmot, Earl of Rochester (1647–80) English poet at the court of Charles II; famous for his bawdy poetry.

The Artists

Franz von Bayros (1866–1924) German painter and illustrator.

Aubrey Beardsley (1872–98) English Decadent illustrator, contributor to the *Yellow Book*.

Antoine Borel (1743–1810) French artist.

Carl Breuer-Courth Early twentieth-century German painter and illustrator.

Jaques Philippe Caresme (1734–96) French artist.

Agostino Carracci (1557–1602) Italian painter and engraver.

Lovis Corinth (1858–1925) German painter.

Theo van Elsen Indonesian-born illustrator working in Paris in the 1930s.

Peter Fendi (1796–1842) Austrian artist, court painter at Vienna.

Henry Fuseli (1741–1825) Swiss-born British artist.

Paul Gavarni (1804–66) French illustrator.

Giulio Romano (1492/9–1546) Italian Mannerist painter and architect.

Gustav Klimt (1862–1918) Austrian artist, leading figure in the Vienna Secession, the Austrian *art nouveau* movement.

Julius Klinger Twentieth-century German artist.

Henry Lemort Early twentieth-century French artist.

Martin van Maele Early twentieth-century Belgian engraver.

Johannes Martini (1866–early twentieth century) German artist.

Louis Morin (1851–early twentieth century) Belgian painter.

Joseph Ortloff Early twentieth-century German artist.

Paul Paede (1868–1929) German artist.

Georges Pavis Early twentieth-century French artist.

M. E. Phillipp German engraver active at the beginning of the twentieth century.

Leon Richet Late nineteenth-century French artist.

Félicien Rops (1835–98) Belgian painter, engraver and illustrator, a leading Decadent artist.

Thomas Rowlandson (1756–1827) English painter, illustrator and caricaturist.

Mario Tauzin (1910–) Parisian artist.

Utamaro Utagawa (1753–1806) Japanese woodcut artist, one of the greatest of his time.

Marcel Vértes (1895–1961) French artist.

Mihály Zichy (1827–1906) Hungarian painter and illustrator.

Sources and Acknowledgements

Bibliographical details of the excerpts in this anthology are given below, with copyright notices and permissions indicated where appropriate. Every effort has been made to acknowledge the copyright owner of the material used. If any excerpt has been inadvertently omitted, the copyright owner is invited to contact Eddison Sadd Editions, the compilers.

Page 9: W. H. Auden, *Lullaby*. From *Collected Shorter Poems 1927–57*, © 1940, 1968. By permission of Faber and Faber Ltd, London.

Page 10: William Blake, *Visions of the Daughters of Albion*. c. 1793.

Pages 10, 11, 124, 125: Vatsyayana, *Kama Sutra*. Trans. Burton and Arbuthnot for the Kama Shastra Society, London. (Also published by Unwin & Hyman, and Hamlyn.)

Pages 11, 23, 58, 87, 94, 101, 125: Poems of Amaru and Mayura from the Sanscrit; Geisha Songs from the Japanese; song from French Indo-China, trans. E. Powys Mathers in

Eastern Love, privately printed in London, 1920s.

Pages 12, 13, 16, 48, 68, 71, 119, 128, 131, 134: Frank Harris, *My Life and Loves*. © 1925 Frank Harris, © 1953 Nellie Harris, © 1963 by Arthur Leonard Ross as Executor of the Frank Harris Estate. Copyright renewed © 1991 by Ralph G. Ross and Edgar M. Ross. Used by permission of Grove Press, Inc., New York.

Page 17: e. e. cummings, *may i feel said he*. From *Complete Poems 1913–1962*. By permission of MacGibbon & Kee, an imprint of HarperCollins Publishers Limited, and Liveright Publishing Corporation, USA.

Page 17: Henry Miller, *Plexus*. Copyright © The Estate of Henry Miller. Reproduced with permission of Grove Press, Inc., New York, and Curtis Brown Group Ltd, London.

Page 19: Robin Skelton, *Because of Love*. By permission of the author and McClelland & Stewart, Inc, Canada.

Pages 21, 43: 'Walter', *My Secret Life*. British Library; reprinted by Grove Press, Inc, New York.

Page 24: Paul Verlaine, *Anointed Vessel*. From *Femmes Hombres/Women Men*, trans. Alistair Elliot, published in 1979 by Anvil Press Poetry, London; Sheep Meadow Press, New York.

Pages 24, 73, 81, 109: *The Boudoir: Voluptuous Confessions of a French Lady of Fashion*. British Library. (Also published by Star Books/W. H. Allen, London; Grove Press, Inc, New York.)

Page 27: Algernon Charles Swinburne, *Love and Sleep*.

Pages 29, 45, 64, 67, 107, 117: John Cleland, *Fanny Hill – Memoirs of a Woman of Pleasure*. British Library. (Also published by Penguin Books/Mayflower.)

Pages 35, 106, 145: Nicolas Chorier, *Satyra Sotadica*. 1660. English trans. in British Library, 1682, 1740, 1786; original in Bibliothèque Nationale, Paris.

Pages 36, 114, 115, 147: Casanova, *History of My Life* (*Memoirs*). Trans. W. R. Trask. By permission of Penguin Books Ltd and Harcourt Brace Jovanovich, New York.

Pages 40, 102, 113, 152: Boccaccio, *Decameron*. Trans. J. M. Rigg for Navarre Society. (Also published by Penguin Books.)

Pages 52, 60, 64, 80: D. H. Lawrence, *Lady Chatterley's Lover*. Reprinted by permission of Laurence Pollinger Ltd, London, and the Estate of Frieda Lawrence Ravagli. Published by Penguin Books.

Page 55: Ikkyu, *Kyounshu*. Trans. Don Sanderson.

Pages 55, 86, 87: Kalyana Malla, *Ananga-Ranga*. Trans. Burton and Arbuthnot for the Kama Shastra Society, London. (Also published by Hamlyn.)

Page 58: Pablo Neruda, *Lone Gentleman*. Trans. N. Tarn. From *Selected Poems* by Pablo Neruda, ed. Nathaniel Tarn, © 1970, by permission of Jonathan Cape Ltd, London.

Page 62: D. H. Lawrence, *New Year's Eve*. By permission of Laurence Pollinger Ltd, London, and the Estate of Frieda Lawrence Ravagli.

Page 71: Ernest Dowson, *Days of Wine and Roses*.

Page 72: Pierre de Ronsard, *Corinna in Vendôme*. Trans. Robert Mezey. From *The Penguin Book of Love Poetry*, 1973, by permission of Penguin Books Ltd.

Page 77: Paul Verlaine, *A Brief Moral*. From *Femmes Hombres/Women Men*, trans. Alistair Elliot, published in 1979 by Anvil Press Poetry, London; Sheep Meadow Press, New York.

Pages 78, 79, 129, 143, 146: Anaïs Nin, *Delta of Venus*. ©

Anaïs Nin 1969, © The Anaïs Nin Trust, 1977. By permission of Penguin Books Ltd, London, and Harcourt Brace Jovanovich Inc, New York. Published 1990 by Penguin Books.

Pages 83, 129: James Joyce, *Ulysses*. Copyright 1934 and renewed 1962 by Lucia and George Joyce. Reproduced by permission of Random House Inc.

Pages 84, 135: Henry Miller, *Tropic of Cancer*. Copyright © the Estate of Henry Miller. Reproduced with permission of Grove Press, Inc, New York, and Curtis Brown Group Ltd, London.

Pages 92, 93: *Chin P'ing Mei*, trans. as *The Golden Lotus* by Clement Egerton, 1939. By permission of Penguin Books Ltd, London.

Page 96: *The Song of Songs* (*The Song of Solomon*). From The Bible.

Pages 98, 155: Sheikh Nefzawi, *The Perfumed Garden*. Trans. Richard Burton for the Kama Shastra Society, London. (Also published by Hamlyn.)

Page 103: C. P. Cavafy, *One Night*. Trans. John Mavrogordato. By permission of the C. P. Cavafy Estate and The Hogarth Press, London.

Page 108: John Wilmot, Earl of Rochester, *A Ramble in St James's Park*.

Page 122: Christina Rossetti, *Goblin Market*. 1862.

Page 124: Sigmund Freud, from *Complete Works*, trans. and ed. James Strachey. W. W. Norton Co., New York.

Page 132: Octavio Paz, *Touch*. From *Configurations*, trans. Charles Tomlinson. © 1968 Octavio Paz and Charles Tomlinson. Reprinted by permission of Laurence Pollinger Ltd, London.

Page 136: Pauline Réage, *Story of O*. Published by Société Nouvelle des Editions J.-J. Pauvert, Paris, 1954. (Also published by Corgi, London.)

Page 138: Oscar Wilde et al., *Teleny* or *The Reverse of the Medal*. 1893. British Library. (Also published by Grove Press Inc, New York.)

Page 139: C. P. Cavafy, *He Came to Read*. Trans. John Mavrogordato. Reprinted by permission of the C. P. Cavafy Estate and The Hogarth Press, London.

Page 151: Edward Sellon, Letter to H. S. Ashbee. From *Index Librorum Prohibitorum* by Pisanus Fraxi, ed. H. S. Ashbee. British Library.

Page 155: Robert Graves, *Down, Wanton, Down!* From *Collected Poems 1975*. By permission of A. P. Watt Ltd, London, on behalf of the Trustees of the Robert Graves Copyright Trust, and Oxford University Press, New York.

Page 156: D. H. Lawrence, *Fidelity*. By permission of Laurence Pollinger Ltd, London, and the Estate of Frieda Lawrence Ravagli.

Thanks are also due to the staff of the British Library and the Bodleian Library, Oxford.

The great majority of the illustrations in this volume (including the front cover picture, *Leda and the Swan* by Heinrich Lossow) are reproduced by kind permission of the Klinger Collection, Nuremberg, Germany. Eddison Sadd is also grateful to: the Naturhistorisches Museum, Vienna, for the Venus of Willendorf (page 7); the Graphische Sammlung Albertina, Vienna, for Gustav Klimt's *Reclining Woman* (page 8); the Noel Rands Collection (page 140).

---◊---

Another fantasy by
Theo van Elsen.

---◊---